How Deep Is The Grave?

Part One of

THE
L I ZARD
TA ES

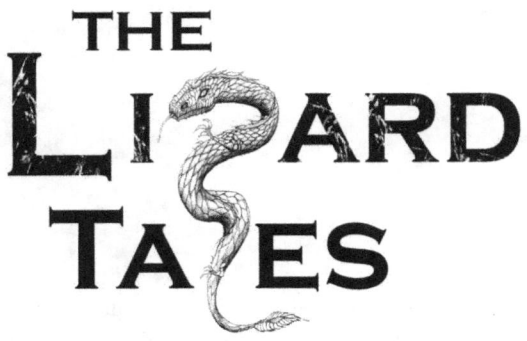

Supernatural Thrillers for Young Adults

Stuart Cresswell

Published by TinselTown Productions

First published in 2011

TinselTown Productions

ISBN: 978-09878646-0-4

Dedications

To the people who have believed in me for so long:
Josephine, for all the love and strength, I hope this goes some way to
making you feel it was worthwhile.
Oliver and Charley, for being two boys that have inspired
me in so many ways.
Roy and Edna, just wanted to make you proud.

THE LIZARD TALES

By

Stuart Cresswell

A series of supernatural thrillers for young people.

The stories are mainly based around the Lizard Peninsula in Cornwall, an area rich in myth and legend. The strong subject matter and stories with a variety of characters widens the appeal to a much larger and international audience. The action also moves to the new world, as the characters find their lives – and their destinies - ever more connected.

"The Lizard Tales" is alive with connections to the 'World Worm' of Norse mythology and full of settings and characters that step right out of Cornwall's colourful heritage.

Each 'tale' has its own set of characters and heroes. Apart from having to tackle the supernatural situation they find themselves in, they have personal problems or difficult choices of their own to contend with. As each story unfolds, the characters find their 'battles' are part of a war being fought against the Serpent and its servants. They also develop strong bonds with each other, becoming a fellowship that must fight a final battle on Saint Michael's Mount.

"With the interesting setting, the strong conflict, and the supernatural overtones, this certainly has the makings of a dynamite series for young adult readers."

Gary Blackwood, Author, "The Shakespeare Stealer" series & "Second Sight."

ACKNOWLEDGMENTS

Re-writers like me rely on someone with exceptional reading and English language skills and the ability to proof-read, edit and comment. I believed that to get best value I'd have to marry a person with those skills – so Josephine, thank you. For everything.
We also need the support of fellow writers to keep us going, and I'd like to thank Gary Blackwood – another north shore Nova Scotia immigrant – for taking the time.
Writers use words to paint pictures, I have always been envious of those who can paint – and paint well. We also need illustrators to help us to visualize our ideas and I have to thank Anna Robertson-Davis, for patience and for wonderful artwork.

Thank you.

～～～CHAPTER ONE～～～

Return and Rebirth

In Pre-Christian and many far-Eastern belief systems, the snake or serpent represented immortality or rebirth, due to the shedding and renewing of its skin.

The ghosts of past places flickered before him as his forehead tapped sleepily on the car window. His eyelids pressed heavily down and houses, trees and people merged into one another as the car made its way back to the hotel through the winding roads of Cornwall. Soon the houses and people were few, replaced by tall hedgerows on either side of ever narrowing lanes.

"David! Don't do that, you'll give yourself a headache." Mrs Givens had a look of real concern on her face. In response, David lifted his head from the window and glared at the back of his father's head.

"I have a headache now." He hadn't, but he knew it would get him his own way.

"Really?" David's mum turned and looked into his eyes, giving him the sort of triage that only mums can do. "You don't look well."

"It's that music. It's too loud." *And it's rubbish!* He thought. *Why do adults think it's cool to listen to Rod Stewart?*

"Turn it down, Cliff." She pleaded with her husband. Although Mr Givens was already turning the car stereo off, David could tell he was not impressed.

"It's not the music. He's been banging his head on the window for the last twenty miles."

Result! Thought David and continued looking out of the window.

"How far to the hotel?" Mrs Givens asked her husband, her concern for David apparent in her tone. Mr Givens shrugged in reply but he cast his own glance to the westward sky and the fading sun. The tall hedgerows blotted out the sun, which appeared only briefly through occasional gate openings or lower hedgerows.

David guessed it would be a long time before they arrived at the hotel. They never arrived on time. His dad drove too slowly. And then there was the long delay before setting off this morning. David had caused that.

His parents had thought they were being clever. He knew they had been guided – or misguided – by Doctor Campbell. He could imagine him telling them: "Plan your holiday, don't tell David where you are going. Lie if you have to. Just get him to Cornwall."

David pulled himself inwards, sleep moving over him. He grinned to himself about the fight he'd put up this morning when he finally learned where they intended to go. He had capitulated. But how they would pay every minute of this 'holiday'.

For a second, his eyes caught sight of a pale, grey shadow of a young boy at the side of the road. In the same instant, his nose sensed salt air and a cool breeze fluttered the hair on his neck. His heart skipped a beat. David didn't recognise the boy – but every part of him 'knew' the boy and he made to reach out to him through the car window, his mouth forming words that stuck in his throat. His finger tips felt the cold of the glass – surprisingly colder than he expected. The car slowed for a bend and David craned his neck so he could still see the boy.

David's eyes strained as the boy faded into wisps of grey smoke and was swallowed up by the shadows of the thick hedge. In his place, David saw two flame-red ellipses, a pair of eyes burning with hate and malice. His brain recoiled from the vision denying what he was seeing. The eyes glided towards the car in a heartbeat and clattered into the window directly in front of David's terrified face.

"Welcome home!" The voice gouged its way to the pit of his soul and clawed at his being.

"Dad!" David's scream was cut short as his head smashed into something hard and unyielding. The car skidded to a halt and his parents turned to look at him.

"What was that thud?" Mrs Givens tried to fix David but he didn't look at her. Her husband leapt from the car and walked behind the car, checking for dead or injured animals. "Did you see anything, David?"

David turned to look at her, his forehead aching and his mind racing, confused, fearful. His dad returned to the car and popped his head inside, giving David a sideways glance as he did so. "There's a dead seagull at the side of the road, we may have hit that, though it looks like it's been there for a while."

He got back in behind the wheel. Mrs Givens looked at David, her face full of concern. Her husband picked up on her feelings. "David?" He said, turning to his son, "what happened?"

David looked at them both; he felt the colour coming back to his cheeks. "I saw...it felt like..." That was the best he could do.

"I know what happened," said Mr Givens, starting the engine, "when the car hit the bump in the road, his head hit the window." The car pulled away and David tried to gather his thoughts, to argue with him, but each turn of the wheels took him further away from the certainty of the event. "Am I right?"

David said nothing. Perhaps that's what happened. It had been a long day. He was tired, seeing all sorts of strange things. This one he would let them have. There would be plenty of time to make their holiday miserable later.

Outside, the scenery looked vaguely familiar. He wasn't sure if he'd seen this landscape before or not. Yet he felt that he knew it, as if from a distant dream. 'Welcome home!' It was just a waking dream, that's all. He convinced himself to forget it.

Then his nostrils twitched in reaction to the smell of the sea, strong and clear this time, carried on a warm evening breeze. Through his father's open window he could even hear the crashing of the waves. The lane reached a small crest and the hedge dropped away to reveal the nearby coast. The wind gusted over the land and the smell of the sea was stronger than ever. As far as he could see, sparkling foaming crests were glistening in the falling sun.

As David had predicted, they checked in to the Royal Albert Hotel too late for a meal. Mr Givens went to great lengths to persuade the hotel owner that there must be something they could eat and the family went to their rooms with a number of filled baguettes and sandwiches.

David let his mother unpack his case for him and watched as she made sure his clothes were neatly hung in the wardrobe or laid in the drawers. He switched the TV on and grunted once or twice as his mum left the room with her customary backward glance just to make sure he was still safe.

He wasn't sure how long he'd been asleep. He heard a voice, speaking softly, over the sound of crashing waves. "The Lizard sticks out into the Channel so far that it is the biggest ship trap in British waters. In fact, so many ships have fallen victim to the Lizard's cliffs and underwater reefs that the Admiralty advises navigators to keep three or more miles off in any kind of rough weather. Those who failed to take that advice have made the Lizard a Mecca for today's wreck divers. The wrecks of the Lizard are of all ages. Some contain real treasure. Not just book talk of silver and gold, but real, hands on, in-the-diver's-palm, silver coins and ingots. Much has been recovered. More is still there to be found by the lucky Lizard diver."

David opened his eyes a little more an tried to regain his sleepy senses as the TV programme continued. He watched as divers combed the sea bed for artefacts or booty. He yawned, stretched and felt a chill which he instantly knew was strange as he was still fully clothed. He could hear other voices, his parents next door, he thought, but then he stopped and listened more intently. Not voices from next door, but whispers in this room. He grabbed for the TV remote beside him on his bed and his hand slapped into a puddle of cold water.

Before he knew what was happening water cannoned into his back and swept him off the bed. He floundered, gasping for air and his body stinging from the cold water. *This can't be happening!* He thought, trying to see evidence of his hotel room. He tried to put his feet down. *The floor must be there somewhere!* Instead another wave turned him over and pulled him down. Down.

David could feel the wet rocks under his body, jagged and cold as he lay on his back. His eyes strained to see through the darkness; darkness that absorbed all light and yet to him appeared to be green and not black. Green so dark and heavy it was oppressive. Behind him, out of his sight, he could hear the rhythmic dripping of water on stone.

David tried to move but he was pressed into the rock by the weight of an invisible force. Drips of water fell onto his forehead. He opened his mouth to cry out for help but he felt it fill with water. He gasped for breath as the drips became a cascade of water on his face.

Drowning!

"No!" He cried out, gulping in mouthfuls of saltwater that made him instantly vomit. Through the dim green darkness he saw the grey shape of a boy tangled in chains of seaweed. He struggled to reach the boy, to untangle his trapped limbs. "I can save you!" He heard himself say.

Then another voice. **"But that's not how it happened!"**

The boy heard the voice too and tried to reassure David, to convince him to keep trying, but as David watched, the boy was pulled further down into the fathomless depths of black-green ocean. Beyond reach. Beyond sight.

"That's not how it happened…" David repeated over and over. He felt the plastic of the TV remote in his hand and cleared his eyes of saltwater. The TV was still showing a program about diving. His room wasn't full of water. The only things wet in here were his trousers. He hated himself.

~~~~

He appeared like an apparition in his parent's doorway. He'd washed and changed into his pyjamas but he had no idea what to do with his wet trousers and underpants. He stood offering them as proof of what bad parents they were.

He could tell his mother felt guilty and he let her fuss around him, taking his wet clothes from him. When she had finished he walked himself back along the short landing to his room. He paused for a moment to listen to his parent's raised voices. He managed to smile, happy that they should suffer too.

"Doctor Campbell doesn't know everything, Cliff..." he heard his mother say.

"I'm aware of that. But he's not the only one. What about Doctor Hamani? And all of those sessions with Oliver? He's a specialist! A child psychologist!"

"But they didn't say it was going to be like this. This is worse – far worse than I thought it would be."

David folded his arms to keep out the chill. He used the landing wall to support his back and his eyes opened up the darkness around him. The hotel was still, sleeping. The only sound was the muffled voices of his parents, and somewhere in the depths of the hotel he could hear the creaking of wood. The hotel was over a hundred years old. The timbers and stone of its beams and foundations were settling down for the night, drifting to sleep in the changing temperatures.

Behind him, he could feel the wall, wood panelled to the height of his waist, then a rich, flock wallpaper, deep burgundy in colour he'd noticed when they arrived. Now, in the tiny slivers of light that his eyes were using, the patterns on the wallpaper made Chinese masks to float around him, dancing like Dragons at a street festival; tongues of flame licking the air as they shuffled past him.

He inched his way back towards his parent's door. Still they argued, still their whispered voices failed to disguise the pain they both felt. David could see them now, sitting up in bed, his dad trying to read while his mum wanted to talk, his father running a finger through his thinning hair, remembering the long struggle they had had to rid David of his nightmares. It had taken its toll on all of them. His mum's face already dotted with drying tears.

"We have to do this, for David's sake." His dad. He didn't change. There was something wrong so he had to fix it. He was the same with everything. His car. His toaster. His shed door. His son. Except there was no manual for David, there were no online instructions. Still he couldn't let it go. And in that there was the heart of his frustration. His son was broken – and he couldn't fix him.

"Cliff. I know, but whilst David still suffers it's as if I can't break away from that…that tragedy."

"None of us can."

David felt a pang of sympathy, felt an urge to burst into their room and hug them both. Instead, he buried the feeling under a scowl, his outward reminder to the world that he suffered. He suffered every day; he had no one to kick out at other than his parents. He started to walk across the landing back to his own room.

He became aware of someone watching him and he looked up to see a face hurriedly pull back from a narrow door opening and be swallowed up by the dark of the room behind. He had already worked out it was the door to the bedroom of Mr and Mrs Kirkman, the owners of the hotel. He thought their names were Mr and Mrs Kirkman, but he couldn't be sure. *They were just being nosey,* he thought.

He looked at the gap under their door. A pale sliver of light flickered and dimmed, as if someone were standing behind the door. Then the light went out and his eyes relied once more on the pale glow from distant appliances and safety signs.

Then he heard a noise from downstairs. He edged closer to the landing edge and held a spindle in each hand, guiding himself to his knees and daring to look further down into the darkness, pulling his face closer to the rails. He heard the noise again. A scraping sound, deep below the building, as if the sleeping hotel were shifting in its bed.

Light picked out only a sliver of the hall below, the tiled floor and part of an antique bureau, an ornate chair. The rest was left to the imagination. David knelt and pressed his face between the spindles and tried to see what was making the scraping noise.

His ears pounded at the silence in the hotel. His eyes strained against the darkness. He held his breath waiting for the noise again. The drumming of his beating pulse roared around the landing, echoing from the flock walls and panelling.

On the verge of giving up, believing he'd imagined it, his senses relaxing, his fists releasing their clench on the spindles, his held breath drifting through his dry lips, the sound of scraping barked through the lower part of the hotel with a crispness of clarity that startled him. His eyes detected a new light source below and he was certain he caught sight of something in the sliver of light – the swirling folds of billowing material, a cloak or long coat. His heart missed a beat. And then after what seemed an eternity of tension, a shrouded figure shuffled into the hall below. In the dim light, David watched as the head turned upwards and revealed a huge face.

In an instant David saw the swollen lips and bulbous nose, the thick rim of bone that lined the top of the eyes that hung heavily into the cheeks. The proportions were all wrong! David recoiled in horror at what he had seen and an audible gasp escaped his mouth. The face vanished back into the shadows and from behind him he heard a noise and he turned to see the Kirkman's door click shut.

David pressed his own door shut and held it there with his back while he caught his breath. This he could do without!

~ ~ ~ ~

Two days passed without incident. Any at all. David spent as much time as possible in his room watching TV. Occasionally they all ventured out into the hotel grounds, but no one wanted to push further afield. It was as if everyone was just biding their time.

His parents were easy with him, though David partly sensed they were holding back, waiting for the right time to push him again. It did occur to him though that his mother had won the argument with her husband for once and for all. That there was no point to this exercise, now or ever. His dad could concentrate on mending those things there was hope of fixing, the dripping taps, the shed window. Those jobs that required the tools his father possessed. He could never fix David. If he could accept that, then David was prepared to accept the lack of words between them. A kind of truce. Uneasy but it would last a lifetime.

Yet they still had him at a disadvantage. He was still in Cornwall. He couldn't relax here. He had to remain on guard. His parents were tricky, treacherous. They had proved that in the past. Whilst there was a chance they had admitted defeat, come to the conclusion that the past was best forgotten, he also knew that the past had been very much returned to him and would remain so as long as he was here.

David woke on the third morning and showered and dressed for the day. He had expected that bags would have been packed by now and they would be heading home, but clearly his parents had decided to be particularly selfish and stay here for their own enjoyment, even having apparently admitted that any hope of 'curing' David was gone.

He had developed a taste for the cooked breakfasts the hotel offered, and found himself having to work a little harder to maintain his mask of world hate. Before long, David had regained the impregnable sullen appearance that he had perfected over recent years. He could sense his parents' awkwardness and was happy to maintain the pressure on them. *Anyway, what do they expect?* He thought, as he sat in silence forcing a third bowl of cornflakes into his eager mouth. *Adults think they know everything. Parents... doctors...they know nothing. Not about me anyway. And I'm not going to tell them anything!*

Once or twice his mother caught him scowling at her across the table. She must have mistaken his scowl for a look of admiration or affection, because she smiled warmly at him. He grimaced, swearing to himself to check his scowl in the mirror at the next opportunity – it might need altering.

He decided until then to not look at them at all, so he scoured the room for something interesting. It pleased him to confirm there was nothing.

That wasn't entirely true. Two things in this room had caught his eye before. The first was a picture. An old photograph in a dark frame. He already knew it to be St. Michael's Mount. A small island that rises up from the waters off the coast of Cornwall, but remains connected to the mainland by a causeway at low tide.

The picture had caught his eye as early as the first morning. Since then he'd found himself drawn to the distinct cone-shape and the chapel that sat at the top. He managed to prevent his eyes from looking into the water that surrounded it but the sea appeared flat, washed to oblivion by the art of the photographer, or the age of the print.

And there was a second thing that had caught his eye in this room. But it wasn't here now...

He grunted to himself.

Although he sat facing the window, David avoided looking out of it. The hotel was set in its own grounds, with trees and hedges and a variety of dense shrubs that provided a view that could have been almost anywhere in rural England. Yet David knew that the sea wasn't too far away. He hadn't seen it; he didn't need to. He could smell it. *Of all the places to come back to!* He cursed adults and their interference. His life was enough of a struggle already, without their help.

"Good morning!" David turned around. *Great! I've got the sea out there, and an annoying Aussie family in here!* He pretended to smile back at Mr and Mrs Carswell, who had arrived yesterday and were already very friendly with his parents. He finished his cornflakes quickly and pondered briefly about the benefits of eating a fourth bowl.

The Carswells stood close to his parents while they chatted briefly, eventually sitting down at the next table. He noticed how his parents smiled now the Carswells were here. He detested the Carswells even more. The pleasant distractions of some new friends would prevent them from worrying about him every waking moment. He could sense he was slipping out of their front minds, the part of their brains he had inhabited for so long, to be placed firmly in the back of their minds, where the rest of life's little inconsequences diminish to nothing.

"I'm going up to my room to watch some TV." He was almost to the door before he'd finished speaking. It didn't matter; the 'olds' were already deep in conversation.

His hand caught the brass doorknob and he gave it a tug. For a spilt second he felt the air leave his body. He was sure there must have been a clearly audible whistle as the breath escaped him. His head fell back slightly and a sensation similar to that of a gentle electric shock coursed through his arm. Gathering himself he watched as the door opened slowly, his hand still on the ice-cold doorknob. The skin on his hand and arm turned white as a ghost and he felt as though it was becoming thinner; he half expected it to tear from his bones as he watched. Yet he was unable to move. Eventually, after what seemed an eternity, the door opened and a girl appeared from the other side of the now fully open door. She looked surprised to see him standing there, but her smile put him instantly at ease.

"Sorry..." he mumbled, apologising for simply opening the door at the same time as the girl. Life returned to him slowly and he felt dizzy from the sudden rush of it.

Great! He thought. *Everyone will think I'm embarrassed 'cause of this girl!*

He noticed that her hand was still on the doorknob, and so there they were, their hands separated only by the width of the door. She was the daughter of the loud Australian couple. Meal times had already been extremely uncomfortable as he had no desire to make conversation with anyone, least of all an Aussie. He had it made it plain since the first time the two families had met, that he wasn't even going to make eye contact with her. Yet now here they were, touching the same piece of brass, albeit through the wooden body of the door. The dying sensation of electricity shivered along his arm and for a while they simply stared into each others eyes.

"No problem," the girl said finally. David pulled the door wider and she manoeuvred past him. He grunted something and then ran all the way to his room.

Two things. The picture of St Michael's Mount. And the Australian girl.

~~~CHAPTER TWO~~~

The Double Helix

Certain facts exist in human history and these are most often found hidden in myths, the common roots of global belief systems providing evidence of these truths. Is it then a coincidence that the depiction of the double helix that represents DNA is remarkably similar to the ancient depiction of the serpents guarding the world tree, a symbol that is repeated in many ancient cultures?

Truddi Carswell walked over to her parents' table and sat down. Just once she turned her head to the door as she heard it open, expecting...wanting it to be David. She hoped no one noticed. She'd already found out that she was a little older than him, but she was a long way from home, from any home she'd had. This was just another country to her and after Cairns, England was little more than a lifeless, cold yawn. Here she was, stuck in a hotel on Cornwall's Lizard Peninsula with a never ending supply of grown-ups and very few people around anywhere near her own age. This was England! England was just a dim room with tired wallpaper and rain-smears on the windows.

"So Truddi, are you going to catch one of the really big waves today?" Asked Mr Givens.

"I'll try...they're all a bit tame around here!" She didn't mean that to sound quite as quashing as it came out but she was nursing her hand in her lap. Ever since she'd come through the door, her arm had been tingling as if she'd had an electric shock.

He felt it too! She thought. *I know he did.*

~ ~ ~ ~

Mr Carswell helped his daughter to slide the surf board off the roof rack. The sound of crashing waves echoed up the narrow cove and the sky held a promise of rain that the sea believed entirely. Rain didn't matter to Truddi. The swell was good and as a result of the overcast conditions the beach was empty but for a few brave souls.

"Do you want me to carry the board?" Mr Carswell pulled his sweater collar up to keep the wind from going down his neck. He hoped she'd say 'no'. She smiled and obliged him and he gave her a nod of appreciation.

"So what are you and Mum doing today?"

"I think we'll take a drive to The Lizard Lighthouse. Sure you don't want to come?"

She cast him a knowing look. If she had a choice between surfing and walking around some crummy building, everyone who knew her would know the choice she would make.

Everyone who knew her? She watched her father drive away into the grey landscape. He was fifty per cent of everyone who knew her in this country. So many people she had left behind against her wishes, but she was kind of used to it. Cairns in Australia had been home for the longest time of any place in her life. She'd loved it there.

Now they were on their way to another new start in Canada. And on the way, by way of gesture of gratitude to his long-suffering family, Mr Carswell was treating them to a tour of the United Kingdom.

The spray was cold on her face but she soon forgot her woes as she caught wave after wave of grey-white water. She loved the sea. It filled her with energy. Somehow it connected to her friends on the other side of the world.

This was the Atlantic. The waters that pounded against the beaches of Cornwall had left the shores of Canada's maritime coast. Nova Scotia! Soon to be her new home. She licked the salt on her lips. Atlantic salt. It was different to Pacific salt. The sea in Cairns tasted of warmth, tropics, coral and fruit. It was warm! The waves there crashed with the sound of laughter and play.

The water of the Atlantic was confused, raging, desolate. The joyous currents of the Caribbean and the Gulf of Mexico were chastised by the ice cold water of the Arctic. The Atlantic's song was one of loss. She heard it in every crackle of surf that receded from the beach. The Atlantic swallowed ships, swallowed lives. Everyone knew about the Titanic. It hit a lump of ice in the ocean!

It may have been summer but if not for her wet-suit the cold would have lashed her. The beach was completely empty as she finally left the water, her board under her arm. The sea and sky were freezing into one, the horizon was closing in and the sand was being peppered by fine raindrops. She towel dried her hair and wrapped the towel around her body to dry her wet-suit.

She looked around. There wasn't a soul on the beach. In fact there wasn't a soul anywhere. The road that wound its way around the bay was empty. The small ice-cream bar at the front of the beach was closed. *This is a spooky place!* She thought and she pulled her bag onto a shoulder and scooped up the board, making steadily for the road where she was due to meet her father.

He was late. She checked her watch again. She swapped the towel for her jacket and trousers and relished the new warmth they gave. She sat at a wooden picnic table and looked out to sea. The grey mists ate their way up the beach and she watched her footsteps disappear one by one, erasing step by step any evidence she had been there.

Rummaging in her bag she pulled out a cereal bar and devoured it. She felt much warmer now, except for the strange cold feeling that had run through her forearm since the door incident that morning. *That was a strange feeling!* She thought of David and convinced herself that it had been some boyish prank – he must have had some joke handshake shock device, sent a charge through the door knob. *Yes, that was it.*

She pictured his face. He was strangely sulky, more miserable than a boy of his age should look. His hair was cut by someone who didn't want to put up with his complaining much longer. He was about the same height as her but he didn't look as athletic. Then there were his eyes. They were compelling. They gave nothing away, as if someone had painted them on, making them attractive but soulless. But they drew your own eyes to them as if they were pleading for rescue.

About time! Through the gathering fog she saw two red lights making their way along the coast road. Rising up with her gear she started to make her way to the road side. The lights shone brighter through the grey swirls and she considered the speed they were travelling. *Trying to make up for lost time, Dad?* Then: *Take it easy around the corners, Dad, these aren't the wide straight roads of Australia now!*

She couldn't be sure, but the lights didn't seem to be following the road anymore. Her heart skipped. *They're going to crash!* Then the lights were not car lights, they were eyes. Red, glaring, malicious and coming right for her.

She screamed and raised her arm in front of her face as the eyes flew at her. Through the mist a huge mouth appeared below the eyes and a serpent tongue flicked her body like a whiplash.

She found herself gasping for air, fighting a chill that ran through her veins, probing her, investigating her, learning all her secrets. The invisible inquisition left her violated, sobbing and startled. She forced herself to seize back what was hers. She pulled her body straight and took a deep breath. The eyes hovered in front of her, red and glowing then edged closer to her.

"Not worthy!"

The voice mocked her, forcing doubts into her own mind about her abilities, her personality, about the goodness of her soul. The Serpent sniffed at her with its tongue and she felt its judgment like a defamation of her character.

Truddi stiffened her resolve, denied the abuse and reaffirmed her known strengths. The Serpent smacked its lips and retreated someway.

"You are not the one!"

"The one..?" To her surprise, Truddi felt the hurt from that remark. She was not being chosen? For what? She felt the coils slip away from her and her senses returned.

"Still. He comes to me willingly. If he offers you too, then I shall not refuse!

"Who..?" The Serpent was gone, leaving the mists to caress her chilled body. She wanted to cry, needed some kind of release. Her body crackled with abandoned energy. She had been made to feel dirty, worthless, false. The thought of people looking at her now made her want to die of shame. She needed a disguise, a painted on face. Like David…

In her heart she knew the 'He' the Serpent referred to was David. That *he* was coming to the Serpent *willingly*. What did that mean? She fought back the fear, the shame; she searched inside the destruction of her being for something untouched by the Serpent's invasion.

The pain hit her in the stomach, tight from the morning's exercise, doubled her over, her arms clasped around her midriff. Salt water gushed from her open mouth and she choked, finding some composure to continue the retch until her stomach emptied of the foul liquid. She felt her knees buckle but she refused to collapse. Instead, as she straightened herself up, she found strength. She was none of the things the Serpent had said. She was tough.

She looked to her feet and saw that she was standing on exposed rock, weathered by time and elements; a thick band of serpentine rock that coiled into the gentle slope of the hill. She imagined it like a serpent, slithering into the depths of the earth, connecting all the ages of the world, all time, at once.

She saw the formation of the land, the turbulence of ceaseless seas, countless footfalls of creatures and man, all imprinting their life into the rock. She saw ships crack in thunderous seas and skies as black as pitch. She felt the sorrow and watched the tears of the grieving pour like a river into a sea of spittle from drowned and abandoned bodies.

The rush of despair caused her to faint, but she caught herself as she fell and her feet left the polished rock, digging into the cold, wet sand. She trembled as if chilled and bit her salty lip to remind herself of her physicality. Then once more she saw the two red eyes approach and she despaired at the thought of another violation.

The red glowing orbs came to a halt a few metres away.

"Sorry I'm late, Truddi!" Her father's voice came through the fog as he backed the car slowly towards her and popped the boot. It lifted slowly in front of her face and she moved like an automaton, lifting her bag into the car boot. Her eyes tried to pull away from the glowing red lights on the back of her dad's car.

"Don't sulk, Truddi!" Mr Carswell's voice carried an apology, but also concern.

"I'm not sulking. I just feel tired…I guess I overdid it. It turned pretty cold out there."

Truddi sat down in the passenger seat and watched as her father steered away along the road.

"This fog doesn't help does it? I tell you, it's no wonder they need lighthouses around here. Do you know how many ships come to grief off this coast?" She didn't know, but she figured he was going to tell her everything he'd learnt on his tour of the lighthouse. She smiled and laid her hand on his leg.

As she listened to talk of storms and wrecks she felt much better, and rationalising what had happened she decided that she had been cold, hungry and tired.

The Serpent was a figment of her exhaustion. She'd been sick after all, vomiting the sea water she'd obviously swallowed while surfing. Yet still the probing had already made her question herself. Deep inside something stirred; something she had learned during the 'inquisition'. She was lonely. She missed her friends far worse than she admitted to herself before.

So that explained the sensations of fear too. Somehow it was just a manifestation of her sense of loss. *Now I know, I can deal with it!* She affirmed. *I'm tough!*

~~~CHAPTER THREE~~~

Gnawing at the Roots of Reason

Nidhogg is a giant worm that resides near one of the three 'sacred wells', the Hvergelmir or "Roaring Kettle". Nidhogg constantly gnaws at the roots of Yggdrasill ("The World Tree") that supports the world. As an omen of doom, a sign of the coming of the end of the world ("Ragnarök") is when Nidhogg chews its way through one of the roots.

Norse Mythology.

David had watched TV for most of the day. He heard the Carswells leave in the morning and he heard them return late in the afternoon. He peeked through the curtains to see their car arrive, Truddi's surfboard clamped onto the roof-bars. She got out of the car and her hair was a tangled, damp mass of black. It didn't make her look less appealing to him, though.

His breath steamed the window. His reflection, now blurred by condensation, distracted him for a moment. It hovered outside his window like a ghost of himself, his aura escaping the confines of the hotel. Clatters of doors and loud footsteps brought him back to the moment.

"Don't be long getting ready, Truddi, the table's booked for six!" David heard Truddi's mum shout to the girl who was already inside. She was always in a hurry. He thought of her riding some waves on her surfboard and without realising it he began to think about the last time he'd seen the sea. Nine years ago.

Nine years before it had been the ideal holiday. David had just turned six and was inseparable from his older brother, Stevie. They'd both been attracted to the crashing waves in the tiny cove where they spent most of their days.

Each day, David watched in awe as his older brother braved the thundering surf and challenged wave after wave to carry him to shore. David longed to follow but was mindful of his parent's warnings to remain close to the beach. Even here, the tug of the water as it slipped back from the steep shore was enough to cause him to lose his balance and the dark, black rocks that funnelled the foam inwards added twisting undercurrents to each powerful incoming wave. Each wave retreated, subdued, only to join forces with a new wave and assault the beachhead again.

What fun! David yelled his warnings to Stevie of bigger waves coming, although all the time Stevie was very aware of the situation constantly unfolding behind him. He was confident he could time his jumps to avoid the big waves and ride the white water of those that broke behind him. This had been the daily game.

But one day, the sea would have its victory.

David forced himself to snap back to the present day. It was bad enough dreaming about it; he wasn't about to start wading through those memories while he was awake!

The Prince Albert Hotel was built at the start of Queen Victoria's reign and set amid rolling fields, several miles by car from the coast. When it first opened it was known by another name, but at some point in its life it had been renamed 'The Prince Albert Hotel'. David wondered if Prince Albert had actually stayed there, but it didn't matter, soon he was thinking of Truddi again. How many times was this today? He really wanted to talk to her, to spend some time with her, but she was here to spend time in the sea. As he spied on their car through his curtains, the sound of voices on the landing outside his door startled him and he hurriedly pulled the curtain back into place.

The return of the Australians to the sleepy hotel was a breath of fresh air. Everything seemed to lift. He could hear his parents next door, suddenly enthusiastic. He heard the drawers slide open and shut as his dad put away his Sudoku puzzle magazine. He heard the small table dragged across the floor to its correct place in the corner of the room, and on it, his mother's jigsaw puzzle of Neuschwanstein Castle in Germany still nothing more than a coloured rectangular border.

The hotel itself echoed to the sound of feet running up steps, doors slamming, raised voices. Laughter.

"The Carswells are back, love," Mr. Givens said to his wife. David sank back in his chair with the TV remote and pretended not to be bothered. Deep inside though, he was happy that his parents seemed to be getting on well with the Carswells.

David gave it a few minutes, waited for the calm to return after hurricane Carswell had hit, and quietly left his room. He glanced towards his parent's door. It was closed but he could hear them talking. He crept past and along the landing. He wasn't sure of his intentions, but perhaps, just maybe he might accidentally 'bump' into the girl.

He was almost past the owner's room when Mrs Kirkman flung open the door. He was like a startled rabbit caught in the headlights of a speeding car. Before he could make up his mind what to do, Mrs Kirkman made it up for him.

"Oh! David isn't it?" David nodded. "Let me have five minutes, me dear." She spoke with a gentle Cornish accent that David found himself mimicking without realising it.

"What..? What for?"

"Help me with these boxes, would you my love?"

He walked past her into the room and the door closed behind him. Mrs Kirkman was packing items of pottery and tableware into several large boxes. The room smelled of tea and a heavy perfume that he wasn't certain of the origin of. Until Mrs Kirkman brushed past him and closed off one of the boxes with heavy tape, then he knew it was from her neck.

"I've got to get these ready for the postman to pick up. He could be here any minute."

David watched her for a moment, then began wrapping items in squares of bubble wrap then placing them carefully in an empty box.

"It's like selling the family jewels, that's what it is." Mrs Kirkman's heavy fragrance of flowers at once overpowered him and soothed him. She talked incessantly as she wrapped and packed and taped.

"We've been here for twelve years. It's not getting any easier. We should be full at this time of year, but no one's spending money right now. Times are hard. But we shouldn't grumble. We have it better than most."

He nodded in agreement. He'd heard much on the TV about one crisis or another. People all over were finding it hard. But then what did he care? Life had been hard for him. The world wasn't bothered about that. There were no news reports about David Givens. No politicians debated his crisis! He wanted to scowl and grunt and glare at her, but she wasn't really looking at him anyway. Besides, her perfume forced his eyes wide open and made his eyebrows push to get away from his eyes.

"So...you've sold all this stuff?"

"Along with a load of furniture and some pictures?"

"The one of St. Michael's Mount?" He had no idea why he asked that, or why it seemed so important. He felt like a simpleton.

"No. We still have that. I'll sell it to you if you want it!" She was smiling at him but he refused to acknowledge her. Yet when he thought she wasn't looking he studied her more closely. She was a little older than his mum, but obviously took some time to disguise that. Her shoulder length hair was shifting from blonde to grey and her face was round, though not fat.

"Have you seen the Lizard?" She asked. He fumbled over his thoughts and pictured a huge Serpent with red eyes almost immediately. "The Lizard Peninsula? What parts have you been to?"

"Er...no...I...not yet..."

"You don't seem to go out much. There's some lovely little coves and beaches all along here. You should get out and see them."

"I know..."

"Oh look at the dust on those!" She almost slapped a plate from his hands. "We can't send them out like this! And the dust is all over your clothes."

"That's all right..."

Mrs Kirkman found him an apron and placed it around him. She tied it at the back and he looked down his front at the daisy pattern. Mrs Kirkman's perfume must have been fading because his eyebrows began to slip down towards his eyes once more. She stuck a duster in his hand and got him to wipe the plates before wrapping them.

He was just starting to wonder how he could get out of this, when there was a knock at the door.

"Come in!" Mrs Kirkman called as she peeled an address label from a sheet and attached it to a box.

The door opened and in stepped Truddi. David stood before her in a daisy patterned apron with a duster in one hand and a plate in the other. For a moment she seemed taken aback, her expression one of total surprise. She smiled, or was that a laugh? Then she looked past him.

"Mrs Kirkman? Can I have the key to the shed for my surfboard please?"

David remained motionless while the two of them chatted around him. Someone was going to pay for this!

~ ~ ~ ~

Later that night, the two sets of parents sat chatting in the hotel bar. David sat in the adjoining room, a small but grand sitting room, with a piano and several floor to ceiling book cases, full of old books. He glanced up from his hand-held electronic game to check the clock on the wall. *Ten-thirty! What do they find to talk about?*

"They're talking about us, you know!" Truddi seemed to appear from nowhere to answer his thoughts. He sat upright. She moved into the room and with a big grin on her face stood at the mantelpiece and ran her finger along it, raising it up to show him the dust. She winked at him, and even he had to fall into the comedy of the shared moment. He nodded, his face full of embarrassment.

She smiled back at him. "I'll say no more about your apron", she said. He shuffled slightly in the chair. "But the daisies suited you!"

"How do you know they're talking about us?" He should have blushed, shrunk from embarrassment, stuttered, said something stupid or drooled on his chin, as he normally did when confronted by an attractive girl – and she was very attractive – but he didn't. It surprised him just how easily he had spoken his first words to her.

"When you go up to them, they stop talking suddenly and struggle to find something else to say. It makes them uncomfortable. Wanna try?"

David strolled into the hotel bar. The two sets of parents sat together near the bar. As he approached them, sure enough their conversation trailed away and they turned to look at him. Mr Kirkman eyed him from behind the bar, his face overflowing with pity. *Too much of it!* Thought David. A few minutes later David returned to the sitting room with a fresh cola, satisfied that Truddi was right.

"Told you," she smiled mischievously, "I'm Truddi by the way."

"I know." He sat on the piano stool and drank to avoid eye contact with her.

"And you're David!" He nodded in reply. There was an awkward silence, in which each tick of the clock on the wall was a thunderclap. "This is an old place. I bet it's haunted. In fact, this whole country is spooky. You should have seen the fog this afto'. I was on the beach. Have you ever surfed?"

"No!" He stopped her dead. Something in his voice told her not to bother. There was more silence and she rose to her feet, ready to leave him to it and his deep mood. But

David couldn't stand to see her go, not now he'd broken the ice. "But there is a ghost here. I saw it!"

~ ~ ~ ~

David knew how it went. Their parents would have sat in the bar until the early hours, a few drinks and they wouldn't be able to help themselves. The Carswells were nice people; they would have listened politely as his mum and dad opened up more and more, baring their anguish, telling them what a hard life they'd had. They'd feel better for getting it off their chests, but that would be the last they'd see of the Carswells. Who could blame them?

So it didn't matter that he'd made a complete idiot of himself with Truddi. Yes she humoured him, pretended to be interested in ghosts, but how could she be? She was happy, healthy, beautiful and into all things that made for an exciting life. She came from a land where the sun shone even on Christmas day and everyone had a swimming pool in their back yard. Why on earth would she have any interest in ghosts?

She'd been polite. Nothing more. And she'd made up some excuse to go to bed early, just to get away from his morbidity. He'd blown it.

"So there it is," he said to his reflection in the bathroom mirror. "Everyone thinks I enjoy being morose and depressed. I know that's what they secretly think, that I get attention because of it, that I can get out of doing stuff I don't like, and have time off school or fail exams." He squeezed the toothpaste onto his brush. "But if I was normal I could talk to her about normal stuff. Do things with her. Not make her... sick..."

He'd not had a shower. Or a bath. Or run any hot water. It seemed strange then that the mirror in front of him should be steamed up so badly. And he was cold. Yes he only had his pyjama bottoms on, but he suddenly felt his skin freeze. He breathed out and a cloud of vapour left his mouth.

He wiped a space on the mirror with his hand and saw part of his reflection – and the reflection of another boy standing behind him! He turned, startled, but there was no one there. When he turned again to the mirror, the condensation and the boy's reflection had gone. He was warm again.

"Stay…" he heard himself say. Inside he knew who had paid him a visit. His brother. Stevie.

He sank inside once more. As he had done so many times. One every occasion that he'd remembered his brother was gone. Here was the emptiness once more, the pit in his stomach; the cavern in his heart. He had built his life - his salvation - on maintaing barriers. This vision, apparition, had lowered his defences. Enough to stab him through his armour.

He went back to cleaning his teeth, but something at the side of the basin attracted his attention. The toothpaste tube was where he left it, but a trail of toothpaste had been squeezed out and on the dark granite of the vanity unit were two letters in Colgate:

$$s\ t$$

"S..t..?" David whispered the letters. "Stay?" He gulped. Who was he trying to fool? "Stevie?"

~ ~ ~CHAPTER FOUR~ ~ ~

Even the Might of Thor

*The Vikings imagined the world of humans (Midgard
or middle-world) completely surrounded and
supported by a great serpent, Jormungand.
Jormungand was the son of Loki and Loki was the
closest thing the Norse had to a Satan.
One tale tells of Thor combating the Midgard Serpent.
He severs its head but is himself killed by a huge river
of venom that spews from the stricken serpent.*

Norse Mythology

Truddi was up early the next morning. She'd found out
that early morning was the best time to catch some good surf,
and she'd found a series of lanes and paths that got her to an
ideal beach nearby in a short time. A mist clung to the fields
on either side of her, but it was already lifting.

Something made her turn as she walked out of the
hotel gate. A boy's face stared at her through an upstairs
window?   *His room? Was that him?* She stopped
abruptly. Truddi had never been the type of girl to pussyfoot
around. She needed some company. If he was watching from
his window at this time of day he obviously liked her.

Shy or not, you're going to talk to me!

She headed back for the hotel and stood below his
window. It was hard to see clearly, but it looked as though the
boy was peering through the curtains.

"Hey! David!" She was careful not to shout too
loudly. The face disappeared from the window. She didn't
have time for his schoolboy embarrassment. She waited a

moment and called again. Suddenly she felt a cold hand on her shoulder. She turned, instantly.

"Ow! You scared me..!" There was no one there. She shivered, and then, just as she began to recover; began to convince herself she was mistaken, a deep, breathy sound, like a distant crash of waves or someone taking a huge breath through their teeth seemed to ooze out of the ground around her. It was followed by a deep guttural groan, almost from the building itself. In a flash it was gone, leaving Truddi wondering if she'd imagined it. She shook her head and dismissed it all as nonsense. Looking back at the window, she called to the boy again.

"Come down!"

No sooner had the words left her lips than David appeared at the doorway beside her. She was thrown completely off guard and looked again at the window above her. Not David? Not even a boy? A reflection of a tree perhaps?

"Is that your room up there?" She pointed.

"No." He considered for a moment her puzzled expression. "I was in the lobby, I heard you calling my name. I was going to see if there were any books in the sitting room about ghosts..." He began to scowl; more angry it seemed with himself than anything else. "What do you want?" He asked.

"Wanna come surfing?"

Even saying the words lifted her spirits. Remarkable in itself as even she was finding the damp and dreary perpetual grey a little depressing. She allowed herself to look up once more to the window and its reflection of a nearby oak tree.

The boy looked down at his feet. "No!"

How could anyone not enjoy surfing? Truddi leaned the surfboard against the hotel wall. "Why not?"

She couldn't help noticing that he suddenly closed up like a giant clam. She took the opportunity to give him a closer look while he wasn't watching. He was all right. Despite being slightly younger than her, his face seemed older, there were constant lines and his expression was 'hangdog' as she called it. Melancholy. *It's an interesting face.* She thought, though she would have struggled to define what it was that interested her.

If she'd been a different type of girl, that would have been the end of it. She was tough, that had always been said. But she never let go, always got her own way. She was only too aware though, that David was the closest thing to her own age around here. So like it or not, he was going to be company for her, if only for the few days her family were staying around here.

"Well...do you wanna go anywhere? With me?"

He lifted his eyes quickly. "Yes!" Then he suddenly appeared anxious again. "But not the sea!"

"Okay, let's walk into town."

"There will be nothing open!"

"Just a walk...we'll be back in time for breakfast...I've noticed how much you like breakfast!"

"Yeah?" He smiled. She couldn't remember seeing him smile before and it was nice.

"Have you noticed anything about me?" She needed to know.

"Yeah!" Now they both smiled.

~~~~~

Truddi paused for a moment as she put the surfboard back in the shed. Not what she'd intended today, but sometimes you had to compromise, that was the grown-up thing to do. She gave the board an affectionate stroke, then left the shed and locked the padlock.

She'd had time to reconsider. Upstairs in her room she'd realized it had been a long time since she'd taken off her wetsuit while it was dry, unused. Swapping it for jeans and hoodie and the prospect of a day without the sea splashing her face touched a nerve or two inside.

She could change her mind. She could meet him later. But that's not really a compromise. She could lie to him and say she had to go somewhere else first – sneak off surfing and see him afterwards. But that was lying. She wasn't given to lying – and certainly not to someone like David, when his face had brightened so much during their last conversation. His expression and pallor had been grey, the mirror of the Cornish morning. Yet he'd smiled and it seemed infectious. She'd certainly caught it from him and so had the world around them; the sun had found a way through the low clouds and poured over them. No she couldn't lie to him.

So today there was no other way. She would have to spend time with him and ignore the call of the sea. And that was no easy thing for her. She'd had time to consider everything as she spent time grooming her hair, applying subtle make-up, finding the right shoes. All her life she'd lived with the smell of the sea around her. All the places her father's work had taken the family, and there were many, they had all been close to the coast. Their new life in Canada would be no different. Nova Scotia was one of the Atlantic Provinces. Surrounded by sea, almost an island. Their new home would have the ocean as a back garden.

So passing up a chance to surf or swim for no reason other than a sulky boy's change of expression seemed to her like she was letting down an old friend. She fiddled with the clasp of her necklace and checked one last time in the mirror. The sea, like the good old friend it was, would understand.

~ ~ ~ ~

The narrow streets of the small town centre were still damp. The shops were full of 'lures' to pull the tourists in: knickknacks and souvenirs, promises of Cornish pasties and cream teas, useful gadgets for people on holiday, campers and beachcombers. Truddi also noticed at least two surf shacks, selling boards and wet-suits, but nowhere was open yet. Still she could visit later.

They paused for a moment to look at a jumbled collection of seaside trinkets and souvenirs in a shop window. There were resin pots with pirates sitting on the lids; carved wooden seagulls on lumps of grey rock; any number of pictures and books telling tales of Cornwall's romantic history. Truddi was most impressed by a collection of ornaments, barometers and clocks, all in highly polished pieces of the local stone - Serpentine.

"Wow! Can you imagine how much work went into that?" Truddi pointed to a very large working model of a lighthouse, its entire structure carved and polished to show the stone in all its beauty. Suddenly, as she looked at the lighthouse, she felt a sense of recognition, as if she knew the very place the model represented. *That's not it!* Then her eyes strayed beyond the lighthouse to a framed picture on the very back of the window display. *Yes, this I know... somehow!*

"St. Michael's Mount!" informed David, following her gaze and ignoring the picture's title. "There's a picture of it at the hotel."

"I know, but this one looks...different!" She continued to scour the picture; something about it was important to her.

"What about this?" David apparently was immune to the lure of the picture. His attention was drawn instead to a full-scale replica of King Arthur's sword Excalibur.

Truddi though was losing herself in the picture, the lines and shapes, the contrasts of sea and rock and sky, the lines of waves that zigzagged snake-like across the page were hypnotic. She struggled to keep her eyes open and she swayed unsteadily on her feet, her hand reaching instinctively to the window for support. She breathed deeply and bit her lip as a reminder, a wake up call.

What was happening? There was something about the picture that had a profound effect on her. Satisfied she wasn't going to faint and crash through the shop window, she began to investigate further. A lesser person would already have gone to a different window – but not Truddi.

At first, Truddi thought she was attracted by the beauty of the image, the causeway to the island at low tide, the colours in the sky and the stillness of the sea. Perhaps it was those painted lines of waves, creating some sort of optical confusion that affects some people. This was Truddi's father's influence. There was always a rational explanation. He was an Instrumentation Engineer; his life was built on logic and trial and error. Like him, she wasn't given to flights of fancy. There was an answer to everything. Everything could be explained.

As she searched for the right questions that would give her the rational answers she needed, she sensed again a deep growl from the pit of the earth, vibrating through her. A chill tickled the top of her spine and she felt the soft, brown hairs on the back of her neck stand in fear. She looked at the picture and it seemed to swallow her whole and only the sight of a new reflection in the window itself prevented her from falling through it and into the landscape of the picture.

The feelings of emptiness, of anger, hate and depression subsided when her eyes picked out the reflection of the surf shack across the road. *Saved by a surf shop!* Twice in one day now she'd had that strange feeling. That feeling of sinking, drowning, disappearing... *Hunger! I'm hungry!* She thought.

The surf shop broke the picture's hold over her. She glanced over to David, who was oblivious to her struggles and still drooling over the sword. She smiled and looked over his shoulder at the blade. *How do they know Excalibur looked like this?* She thought. She spun him around by the arm and directed his gaze to the surf shop across the street.

"You ought to buy a body-board...it's a great way to start surfing..." Truddi was cut off savagely by David's angry grunt and she was surprised at his ill manners sometimes, but she was prepared to let it go on this occasion. She was just itching to get away from this shop in particular and they had the rest of the street to see.

Shops began to open and people seemed to appear from nowhere to take up the limited spaces in the small cafes serving breakfast. The smell of bacon and sausages reminded David he hadn't had his own breakfast yet. They picked up the pace and headed back to the hotel.

The morning sun was burning its way through the mists. Most mornings seemed to start this way. The air filled with vapour, like the breath plumes of a giant creature.

The lanes that led back to the hotel were lined with high hedges, blocking much of the view, barring the sunlight from reaching them, making the roads feel even narrower than they were. Once or twice they were passed closely by cars, forcing them into the muddy verges as the drivers negotiated the tricky bends, narrow road width and unexpected pedestrians.

Truddi considered the hedge roots at her feet as she stood on the verge and waited for a car to pass. The hedges were countless years old, maybe hundreds of years, the roots were thick giving some indication of age, and they twisted around each other into the dark soil. Stone blocks at the base of the plants struggled to contain the bulging roots. At times large trees, planted among the hedgerow, forced the small walls of stone blocks lining the earth bank to give way completely.

One section was riddled with rabbit holes and Truddi had seen plenty of them on her early morning sojourns. Still, she felt small, claustrophobic, overpowered by the oppressive height and density of the hedges. She wanted a view. She wanted wide open vistas. An ocean at her feet.

They were greeted at breakfast by two sets of smiling parents. The arrival of Truddi and David together was just the excuse the parents wanted and the two tables were rearranged to make one big one and breakfast was to be a noisy, chatty affair from now on. Truddi caught David throwing a glance at her parents, as if he admired them for some reason, and he visibly relaxed as he listened to his parents talking and laughing.

What a strange little boy! She thought.

~~~~

"Sit down, Truddi." Mr Carswell did that thing he often tried to, scooping a chair around to face him and straddling it in one flowing movement. He usually ended up bashing his knee, but this time he sat on it perfectly and rested his elbows on the back rest to fix his attention on Truddi.

She sat down; her mother pulled a chair across and sat down too. Her mind flashed back to the day in Cairns, almost a year ago now, when they sat her down like this and told her about her dad's chance of a new job, what it would mean for them and asked her for her thoughts.

It was an age-old conversation. Mr Carswell had 'wandering shoes' as he called it. He'd grown up in the lowlands of Scotland, where work was hard to come by. An easy option for boys from working class families, where there was no work, was to join the Armed Forces. He'd chosen the Royal Navy. He saw the world, learned a trade, became a qualified Electronic Instrumentation Engineer. To pay for it, as a young seaman he'd seen terrifying action during The Falklands War. It was something he never spoke about.

He left the navy, found work in the new industries growing up at the start of the telecommunications revolution. His skills were in demand. They took him to Europe, working for a company with offices around the world. Shortly after Truddi was born, they moved to Italy. From there within a year they were in Norway, then the move to Cairns in Australia. Truddi had never really been old enough to have a say in those early moves. But her parents had involved her in the move away from Cairns.

She felt now that she had let herself be bought really cheaply. She had given up a lot for them and their professional ambitions. She missed her friends and she missed the sun for sure!

"We have learnt a few things about David," Mr Carswell continued.

Why on earth are they talking about David?

"This is the first holiday that family have had for nine years." As he spoke Truddi noticed that her mum had a tearful look on her face. "The last holiday they took, was near here. David had a brother. He drowned. They all took it really badly."

Truddi was shocked and then as she remembered things David had said or done, she began to understand. Her mum took up the story.

"Not finding the poor boy's body had made their loss harder to bear, they were distraught of course, but David's parents somehow managed to come through it over time, possibly only because of David. They would have to focus on him you see. But it soon became obvious that David was not going to get over the tragedy easily. The loss of his brother - and from what they were saying the boys were really close - well, it all but destroyed David." She ran a finger along the bottom of her eye to scoop away a tear.

"They don't have what we would consider to be a normal family life." Mr Carswell looked keenly at his daughter, watching her reaction, to see if she understood.

"Mr and Mrs Givens lost two sons that day," her mother chipped in and she breathed deeply to gather herself.

"That said," continued Mr Carswell, "everyone is concerned about David. Nine years is a long time to come to terms with what happened. But doctors and specialists can't seem to get him out of the place he's got into. He's afraid of water, the sea especially…"

Truddi knew the sea had to be respected, but she couldn't imagine being afraid of it. Still she listened, wondering what it was they wanted her to say.

"He had been such a lively little boy, happy, fun, full of interests and energy." Mrs Carswell placed a hand on Truddi's hand which sat on her knee.

"But now," continued her father, "it seems everyone has the same idea. All the experts, relatives, friends and newspaper agony aunts think the same thing. He needs to come back to Cornwall, to the sea, and face his fears."

"They never found the brother?" Truddi finally spoke, her own mind racing to find a solution. Her parents shook their heads. "Perhaps he just needs to say goodbye." She sat up straight, fixing them both with that look of determination that was at her core. "I could help!"

Mrs Carswell smiled at her daughter.

"Would you want to?" The words had barely left her dad's lips when she leapt in.

"If we stand by them now, we can't give up on them. It's no good offering kind words today and leaving tomorrow. We can't just push on through."

"You happy to miss out on the rest of your trip?" Mr Carswell wanted to be sure.

"It's your trip too, dad."

"Well, we kind of felt we liked these people anyway. If we'd made definite bookings in other hotels, then maybe we'd have felt differently."

"So we stay here?" Mrs Carswell pulled her daughter in close for a hug. "I'm glad. I don't think we'd have liked ourselves if we didn't try to support these people."

It made total sense to Truddi now that she knew why David had no love of the sea, and from that moment Truddi assumed the role of David's rehabilitator. She was prepared to selflessly abandon her desire for daytime surfing to spend time with David away from the sea.

At times as the next few days passed, her nostrils would sense the sea on some gentle breeze and she'd fidget restlessly. The following morning she'd get up extra early and surf before anyone else was awake.

~ ~ ~CHAPTER FIVE~ ~ ~

The Pit of the Ghoul

*The inevitable path is a thing that is living in
itself, autonomously living. This can be seen in the
Chinese concept of Tao, where Tao was symbolized as a
dragon and that the dragon and the snake are
mythological equivalents. This living path can also be
seen to be Christ: The serpentine way of the individual
is the straightest way he can possibly go. That is
symbolized by the serpentine way of the sun through
the Zodiac, and the Zodiacal serpent is Christ, who
said: "I am the way [John 14:6]". He is the serpent, so
in the early Christian church he is the sun, and the
signs of the Zodiac, the apostles, are the twelve
months of the year.*

Carl Jung.

David struggled to free himself from the seaweed that
bound him tightly to the rock wall. He became angry, well
aware as he slept that this was a dream. He rebelled against
the illusion and heard his brain shout out to the dream itself
that reality must be returned.

So reality returned.

The beach returned.

The beach on the day of Stevie's death. How often
did he think of this? Dream of this? In the early days when he
was forced to speak of the events, how often had he told the
story not as it happened – but how he needed to remember
it?

Reality?

The sea had been clever. It had let the two playful boys believe they were the masters. Day by day, Stevie had become more daring, more confident of his command and knowledge of the foaming surf. David too waded in deeper and deeper, eager to feel the tug of the undertow and the pebbles rolling away from the shore beneath his feet.

David felt happy and proud. Proud that he was almost as daring as his brother. But so very proud of his brother. And pride has always come before a fall.

What sounded like ripples of applause came from all around the cove, as water splashed from rock to whirlpool. Yet these were not cheers for the two boys, but applause for the sea itself, as it made its opening gambit.

David leaped up and down, screaming with delight as his brother emerged through foaming, white sea - shallow triumph in deep water. Stevie was supreme, ever conscious of the mood of the sea, yet to his younger brother, it all appeared more dangerous. This made Stevie appear even more heroic in his younger brother's eyes, a Titan of the waves!

David had fallen first. The retreating wave unbalanced him, putting him in the path of the next incoming wave and all of its force. For a moment, Stevie ignored his own position, and scanned the shore for his beloved younger brother. His concerns vanished as David spluttered to his feet. All was well, but the sea had only just begun to play!

More desperate to wake up from this than the previous visions, David tossed and turned in his sleep. He remembered being under the sea, spluttering, floundering. He remembered hearing Stevie calling, his voice strong and concerned, carrying through the water. This had happened. Why would it never leave him?

Then Stevie's voice became the water, wrapping around him, passing through him, dripping into his ears where it reverberated through his body. He heard the water call his name from below the waves. '*David...*' He saw Stevie, falling ever deeper under the sea, his arms flailing, reaching, stretching and in turn his arms became huge fronds of seaweed that threaded around David's submerged body. He felt them pull him; felt his soul pulled further under the darkening water.

He could do no more, despite fighting it, despite knowing that he couldn't breathe under water, his mouth had to open, already tasting salt on his gums. His lungs banged inside his chest, demanding air. He fought the impulse to gasp, to breathe, knowing that his lungs would fill with water and not air.

In a myriad of moments he felt the salt water enter his mouth; felt the desperate gush from his lungs as they tried to breathe in air; tried to spit out the water faster than it entered his throat; felt himself retching; felt himself screaming; saw Stevie's face right in front of him, angry, bitter, twisted, bloated by nine years of cold water and now bursting open; oozing cloudy sea-water.

Then, instead of seaweed, he felt himself supported by his mother's gentle arms. As his eyes rolled back into place he felt air entering his lungs.

"Breathe deeply," he heard his mother say. For a moment he looked at her, almost told her something that he knew he wanted her to know. But it was too big a thing. He'd never be able to face his parents again. He shoved her away and took himself to the bathroom with the change of pyjamas that his mother had laid out for him. He changed his wet bed clothes in silence, waiting for his mother to leave his room.

He heard the door click shut and he sobbed quietly in anger and shame. Slowly he walked back to his bed and tried to go back to sleep.

~ ~ ~ ~

By the middle of the second week, the change in David was apparent to everyone. Fresh air, exercise and Truddi's infectious energy played their part in giving David far better sleep than he'd had for a long time. He almost looked like a young boy again. Colour was returning to his cheeks.

Colour though had disappeared from the world outside. Into the second week and the morning mists began to linger longer into the day, until, by Wednesday, it didn't disperse at all and the grey moist air sat heavier around the hotel. It rained a few times, but even when it wasn't raining, the dense damp air left everything in its reach coated with a film of moisture.

David and Truddi shook themselves on the doormat like two damp dogs. Less than an hour outside and they'd both been coated in a good amount of fine drizzle. It was going to be one of those quiet days. On holiday in Britain you can always count on getting a miserable grey day or two, one that allows you to do nothing of any great importance - the most exertion that adults put themselves through is ordering another coffee from the hotel bar.

Truddi and David almost joined their parents, but Truddi had noticed one of the downstairs doors for the first time. She manoeuvred David along the corridor, through the breakfast room and into the far corner of the room.

"This is weird!" she said, examining the ancient wood. The door seemed to be part of the original building, but new rooms had been made and walls added to conceal the door along a narrow passage. Normally a large dresser had blocked the passage, which is why they hadn't noticed it before. This morning, the dresser had most certainly been moved. Before David could stop her she had tested the door, found it unlocked and opened it.

A small anteroom, perhaps an old scullery, was what they stepped into. They were just about to turn around and go when they noticed another tiny door. Truddi opened it.

"An elevator!" She said.

"A lift!" David corrected.

They both stood inside and closed the metal doors. Truddi pressed the button at the bottom and the hum of a motor was followed by a gentle jolt and the sensation of descending slowly. The motor stopped and they both looked at each other.

"Basement! Kitchenware, linen, lighting and...er... hats!" Truddi grinned and threw open the doors before David could object.

It was darker than the room they'd been in previously, but there were lights set into the ceiling, giving off a dim, yellow glow. Before them a steep flight of stairs descended beyond view into a large tunnel, its walls neatly covered with white ceramic tiles. Here too were more lights. A thick black cable pressed into the ceiling carried the power and although far from all of the lights worked, the tunnel seemed to be lit well enough to walk safely.

Truddi also smelt the fresh salt air that comes only from the sea. She threw a glance at David and hoped he hadn't smelled it too. No matter. He was dead against going further anyway.

"We can't just go poking around in someone else's house!"

"It's a hotel."

"We're guests."

"So come on - be their guest."

With that, Truddi started down the stairs. David followed, reluctantly, but it was soon obvious there was nothing scary about the tunnel. There were handrails and the steps were carved evenly into the rock. The tiled walls rose up and curved into the arch of the roof, giving plenty of headroom. This quality continued as the stairs ended and the tunnel levelled out. They could tell that this was a structure of quality, probably built for wealthy people of importance that had stayed in the hotel in years gone by, when only the very wealthy stayed in hotels such as this. It would have been a grand way to stroll to the coast.

They hadn't been walking long when they sensed something coming the other way. Instinctively they dived for a recess in one of the walls, and took cover in the darkness. They heard uneven footsteps coming slowly nearer, and the scraping of wood on stone. Shadows danced on the white tiles as the figure passed one light and then another as he plodded towards their refuge.

David heard a man's gasps of breath and Truddi's sensitive nostrils sniffed stale sweat. They each held their breaths, cowering in the shadows. A huge man appeared alongside them and he halted. He seemed to look right at them and light fell across a bulbous face like death itself. He must've been seven feet tall at least and his cold grey eyes searched the shadows - surely he could sense them. Was it the thumping of their hearts? Truddi pressed her chest against the wall, trying to stifle the drumbeats, she felt David squeeze against her, pressing her to the stone as he tried to vanish from the man's sight.

Slowly, the man turned his misshapen head away from them and began to walk again. He pulled behind him a long wooden box. The shape and size of it meant only one thing to Truddi. She sensed David's eyes bulging and knew he thought the same thing. *It was a coffin!*

For an eternity they waited. His irregular footsteps echoed from further and further away, until the scraping became a timid mouse scratching the floor of its cage. Only when they were sure he'd gone, did they emerge from their sanctuary. Neither said a word. Fear gripped them and they hurried back the way they had come.

"What was that?" David tried to appear calm but he was walking far quicker than normal.

"I'm not sure...it probably wasn't..." Truddi stopped. She saw that David had also seen what she was looking at. The scratch marks in the floor made by the wooden box. "That's a heavy box...real heavy!"

"I was hoping I had imagined it." His face registered inner terror.

Their pace quickened in unison without a word.

They reached the foot of the stairs just as the door at the top slammed shut. They stood helpless as they heard a series of bolts and locks clang into position on the other side.

Then they both gasped fearfully as all the lights went out with the echo of the power lever slamming off on the other side of the door clanging around them.

Truddi carefully climbed the stairs, her fingers searched for locks or keys but the door yielded no release mechanisms on this side. She fumbled her way back down to David, who was beginning to find a voice for his panic.

"Brilliant! Now we're stuck! I told you we shouldn't..." But Truddi had no time for this. She pushed past him and using the smooth walls as a guide, she began to feel her way back along the tunnel.

"Where are you going?"

"That...man...came from the other end of this tunnel - so that's where we get out!"

She expected David to argue, so she set off at a swift pace before he had time to formulate an opinion. Truddi had a good idea where the tunnel would emerge - that sea salt smell was getting stronger! She wondered if David could smell it too.

"Where does this go?" He asked, almost to himself. "I'm having a bad feeling about this..."

By the time daylight crept into the dim walkway, his complaining had ceased. She could make out his face in the half light and he looked as though he was going to be sick. Distant sounds of rolling surf echoed around them. Light seeped into the tunnel and the once more visible tiles channelled the sounds of the sea like crashes of thunder, and with each clap David's eyes widened.

The cries of seagulls pierced the dull thuds of the surf, shrill and painful and she saw them wake terror in his eyes. As a seagull's mournful cries penetrated their narrow space, David reached out a hand and clutched Truddi's arm, almost unaware that she was there.

"Stevie?" He whispered. Truddi stifled a cry of sympathy. She watched as his arm stretched out as if trying to save his brother from the noisy foam.

"It's okay. There's a beach. I can see it. I promise you won't have to go in the sea." This was hardly any comfort to the trembling boy. "We have to do this...you'll be all right, I promise." She held his hand with firm reassurance.

They emerged into the daylight. A few stone steps led down to a small sheltered beach, black rocks rose up all around and the cove was enclosed on the shore by several huge rocks. The impression was of a sea cave that had collapsed, and the huge rocks on the beach were now all that was left of the roof or the original cliff face. They stood for a while - a while longer than David wanted to - then stepped down onto the sand. The damp and drizzle had made the sand cold and moist - a deep rusty colour. Truddi noted the tidemark, telling her that the sea usually came in at least to the bottom of the steps.

David kept his head turned away from the sea - he pretended to be looking for a way up the cliffs, which rose steeply, at least fifty metres, so climbing them was going to be difficult. They found a good place to start and Truddi led the way.

Eventually they reached the top of the cliff and fell onto the damp grass, the reality of their ordeal expressing itself in relieved laughter. Then questions buzzed between them, seemingly endless; too many and with no ready answers. *The tunnel? The grotesque man? The coffin?*

"Was it *his* coffin?" Truddi's imagination was rampant.

"No...Someone else was in it...it was heavy."

"He was heading for the hotel. We should tell someone..."

"I saw him!" David told Truddi how he'd been on the landing. "A few nights ago, he was in the hotel. I think the owners know about him. I saw them watching, as if they were expecting him..."

Truddi wiped her hair away from her face. *That was nice, a breeze, might shift this mist.* "So what is he doing at the hotel?" Truddi began to worry. It was likely that plenty of people knew about the tunnel. They could trust no one with this.

They rose to their feet and tried to get their bearings. The tunnel may not have been straight and to Truddi it had felt as though they had walked as if it had curved to the left all the way. The hotel could be in any direction from where they were now.

As they walked, they found out why the cove was bereft of visitors and isolated from other tourists. An electrified fence stretched around, keeping cattle and humans from venturing nearer than half a mile from the steep cliffs. As they slithered between the wires, Truddi noticed a warning sign placed to warn those approaching through the fields on the other side: "Keep out - dangerous cliffs."

"Appreciate the advice!" She mumbled.

The field they were now in looked just like all the others around here, surrounded by tall hedges and without a recognisable landmark anywhere. Yet they agreed they hadn't walked that far in the tunnel.

"The road from the hotel goes to a beach. But this beach must be closer than that one!" David seemed to be doing mental calculations of distance. *Perhaps knowing how close he was to the sea at all times was important to him.*

"I go to a beach near the hotel some mornings," she admitted to David and she was pleased to see his reaction seemed ambivalent. "It's a good walk down the lanes; I go left out of the drive..."

"So?"

"That's the nearest beach, I'm sure. And the land around it looks nothing like this."

"That's what it's like around here," said David. "This coastline is a mass of ins and outs, narrow coves and clefts that cut in from all and any direction. You need a high point to get your bearings." They looked around but the countryside was largely flat. They waded through long damp grass putting distance between themselves and the edge of the cliff.

Before long, they heard the pounding of surf and to their right they found a steep cut in the rock which brought the sea at them from a new angle. David wobbled as if struck by vertigo. Truddi's brow furrowed. *This was getting confusing!*

They came across a small outcrop of black rock and Truddi scrambled to the top. Across the top of hedgerows she caught sight of a familiar landmark.

"Over there!" She pointed. "It's that tower you can see from the road as you approach the hotel from town!"

"It's a tin mine!"

"It's a start point. We can pick up the road to the hotel near there, surely!"

They set off with new purpose picking up a narrow lane on the other side of a thick hedgerow. Eventually they could see the hotel, in a small dip in the otherwise flat area of land. The country lanes wound through the countryside and disappeared behind towering hedges that obscured the view of the hotel from just about everywhere.

Back at the hotel, their parents hadn't missed them, wrapped up in crosswords and Sudoku. They both found it hard not to speak about their adventure. Instead they sat in the sitting room and watched the grey mists begin to lift on the incoming breeze.

David studied a large map of the area on the wall. The roads cut deep into the peninsula from the village of Trelurrion where the hotel was sited, and minor roads also meandered to some of the bigger beaches. The beach they'd just found themselves on was closest of all to the hotel - but only found by trekking along a mile of fields and ditches...or by a tunnel!

Truddi watched his fingers trace the path of their adventure on the detail of the map. *Well, he'd survived being that close to the sea. There was hope for him yet!*

They were both startled by a face suddenly appearing in the doorway alongside the map.

"Been looking for buried treasure?" Mrs Kirkman nudged David playfully, but her smile faded quickly when she looked at Truddi.

She knows! Thought Truddi, as she tried to contain her own expression from giving any more away. But the implication of the woman's words was as plain as the stunned look on Truddi's face.

~~~CHAPTER SIX~~~

Silence of the Snake

Alone among the animals
the snake does not sing.
The reason for them is the same
as the reason for stars, and not human.

Margaret Atwood.

Coming so close to the sea had taken its toll on David. Sleep came uneasily to him, and when he finally drifted off to sleep he woke with a start. Wide awake! The room was too dark to see much of anything, but there was a distinct smell - *fish?* He also felt the room to be extremely cold. *Was there someone in his room?* He sensed there was.

Faint whispered voices tickled his hearing.

"Who's there?" No reply came, but now he was certain he could hear them. *What were the voices saying?* 'Stay above the sea!' *Was that it?* A small line of light always shone under his door from the light on the landing. As he looked at it, the line became a blur, expanding until it seemed to be a whole doorway filled with light. Grey light, as if filled with smoke or dust.

"*Stay above the sea!*" The whispers became clearer, more defined, affirming the rule he lived his life by.

A boy's face became visible near the foot of this bed. He stared right at David, fixing him with cold eyes full of need. The boy looked about nine. To David, there was only one boy this could be. *Stevie!*

"Help me..." the boy seemed to say.

David was almost overpowered by the rank smell. Then he noticed objects on top of his chest of drawers beginning to move. A film of moisture appeared over the mirror, and letters drawn by an invisible finger began to appear on the glass.

$$S\,t\,\mathcal{E}\,v\,i$$

"Stevie!" David's eyes were wide open. The times he'd called that name from deep inside a nightmare - yet this was different. He hadn't been asleep; he was convinced he had been awake. Fully awake. Not confused or blinded by bad memory. The smell was gone and the whispers silenced. The light in the doorway dissipated until all that remained was the landing light under his door. The boy had gone too. David leapt out of bed and onto the landing.

"Stevie!"

As he reached the banister on the landing, he looked into the darkened hall below. A figure, surprised by David's arrival, looked upwards - his deformed features catching the light from the stairs. For a moment they looked at each other, and then the man melted back into the darkness. David staggered backwards, away from the banister and reeled into the wall behind - a terrified wail escaped from the pit of his stomach and cried out its freedom from his lips.

Seconds later, the landing was full of people. David's mum and dad. Mr and Mrs Carswell. An old couple from across the landing. The Kirkmans who were both watching proceedings unfold with some concern apparent on their faces.

David's worried parents comforted him and returned him to his room. Through the fussing folk around him, David searched for the one face he needed to see...Truddi. Sure enough, she was there and even without words, she could tell by his eyes this was no ordinary nightmare. But Truddi would have to wait until morning to find out what was special about it.

Neither family slept well for the rest of the night.

~ ~ ~ ~

The next day was more pleasant. The mist and clouds had cleared and the sun battled its way through from time to time. Little was said at breakfast and both families decided to take a walk along one of the cliff paths. David was notably silent, the mention of sea and cliffs made him outwardly apprehensive - but he also needed time alone with Truddi, to tell her about last night - and they could camouflage their chatter with the leisurely stroll.

"You saw him again?" Truddi found David gesturing to her to keep her voice down. He looked back to the adults, checking for signs that they could hear.

"Yes. He was in the hotel again. He vanished into the shadows as soon as I saw him."

"Mr and Mrs Kirkman were on the landing last night, too. She looked as if she was hatching some sort of plan. We may be in trouble if she suspects we found the tunnel and now she knows you have seen the... whatever-it-is-man." She paused for breath. "What is he, do you think?"

David smiled at her quizzical look. He had seen boys at school, older than him, parading their girlfriends around the campus, or in town. Not one of those girls could hold a candle to Truddi. And she wasn't even trying today. She wore a tee-shirt with the emblem of some rock band he couldn't make out and a pair of shorts made from old jeans. But there was no denying, she was perfect! And right now, he got to spend every day with her.

"Don't worry about the Kirkmans," David urged her to continue walking. "My parents explained to them when we arrived about my nightmares. They have no idea I saw the - whatever-it-is-man - last night. And I kind of get the feeling they don't want him around either. It may be bad for business to have a ghost or...whatever, running around."

"So what is it you are itching to tell me then?" The way Truddi looked at him made him melt. There was a lot he wanted to tell her, but if he ever did, she would run a mile in the opposite direction and that would be that.

"I don't know what that man is," he said, "ghost or what, but there was a ghost in my room last night for certain. And it was Stevie!"

"Are you sure it was Stevie?" Truddi enquired, once David had recounted last night's events at least three times.

"It looked like him...for sure, and he wrote his name on the mirror - just like he used to in the bathroom after a shower - with his finger."

"I do that...so do millions of other kids..."

"But why would another ghost write *his* name? Stevie!"

There was a silence as they clambered over a stile. Their parents were a long way behind, no doubt locked in a psychological study of David and the benefits of having Truddi around.

"Ponies!" Truddi said with barely restrained excitement. She trotted ahead and got herself as close as she dared to the animals. The two of them found a position behind a rock and watched as the small herd of wild Shetland ponies picked their way along the jagged slopes. Their task was simple, to eat the grass along the cliffs and keep it under control. David read the notice board to Truddi which explained all this and requested people not to feed them.

"Horses are my second favourite thing," bleated Truddi.

"What's the first?" David assumed it would be some boy at her school.

"Surfing..." David flinched visibly and she held back, watching his face for signs of trauma. Finally he nodded in understanding and she reached out a hand to his, but he moved his hand away, just enough to make her give up the task. She smiled back but he sensed however that the chasm between them had just grown wider.

"We were supposed to be spending some time in the New Forest," she continued, "they have wild ponies there, too...and then some pony trekking in Northumberland. So I'm glad I've seen some wild ponies anyway."

"So why aren't you going to the New Forest and Northumberland?"

"I...I think mom and dad are having such a great time with your folks here...they've hit it off. Nice, d'you think?"

"Yeah. Not very vice for you though..." he turned away and his face turned melancholy again. Her eyes said: 'It's because of you,' and she quickly avoided his returning eyes. Still he must have read her thoughts. "It's because of me isn't it?"

She stammered which gave the game away instantly to him. She never stammered, never gave any outward signs of nerves. "Well...yes actually..."

"Why? Do you think I'm dangerous? Do you think I need 'special care?' Is that it?" He seemed on the verge of tears, his face filling with rage.

"It's not like that!"

"No? Sounds like my parents have been spreading the word about me again!" He turned to storm off but the sight of the distant sea edging the cliff horizon stopped him quickly. He seemed to lose confidence and he tottered briefly, long enough to conceal tears of frustration.

"Where do you live?" His voice was more controlled, as if he'd sensed that walking away now would send him over the edge - in so many ways. Truddi kept her voice soft, ready to accept and forgive his outburst. Her mouth tightened in contemplation of what it must be like to be the subject of everyone's after dinner conversation.

"We're on our way to a new home in Canada. My Dad travels about with his job. We lived in Italy and Norway. Then we moved to Australia. Three different homes there. That's where I learned to surf. It's a cool place. Canada's going to be different, though. No surfing there! Just ponies, I hope."

"So you don't know the house you're going to live in?"

"It's being built. Hopefully it will be finished by the time we get there." She forced a laugh. "We all had a say in the design of the house." She stopped and looked at him.

He wilted under the scrutiny of her eyes, swallowed by a wave of melancholy bigger than any wave the sea could muster. And he felt sorry for himself, sorry that Truddi could leave at any time, that Truddi had things that she wanted to do more than be with him. He felt her eyes like hands slapping his face to jolt him out of his self-obsession and then in a flash he changed and turned to her smiling, resigned to make what time he had with her as enjoyable as possible.

"Look at that really little one, cute or what?"

"Coool!" She agreed and her eyes softened once more towards David.

From somewhere below them they could hear a dog barking. Truddi leaned over the crest of the cliff, which fell away violently. In a tiny cove, a lone dog was barking frantically at something she couldn't see. What she could see was the sea and the tide was moving in quickly.

She pulled David along with her, down a winding, almost invisible path, which followed a small stream as it in turn followed a narrow groove in the soft topsoil and sandstone. The stream cut its way through the cliff, vertically in places, forming miniature Niagaras cascading to the cove below.

Before they reached the beach, David halted. He could go no further. Now he could see the waves lapping onto the small shore. The dog, still barking towards the back of the beach, seemed to prefer the encroaching sea to whatever was the cause of its distress.

"I'm staying here." David felt like a wimp, but he couldn't fight it. "Save him, Truddi."

Truddi didn't even try to persuade David to follow her. Scrambling down, squatting and slipping on her bottom, clinging to handfuls of tough grass, Truddi descended. Her foot slipped at one point, shooting out from under her and sploshing into a lively stream that ran hidden under overhanging grasses. She muttered under her breath and looked around for other options. There were none. If she didn't reach the dog soon it would drown.

"Why is it so frightened?" She called to David. David scanned the beach. He could see nothing else on the beach, yet still the dog backed towards the sea, barking madly at something higher up the shrinking beach.

"I don't know! I can see right to the cliff and there is nothing there!"

Finally, she was able to drop onto the sand. She shook the water from her shoe and began speaking softly to the dog. She reached the dog and set about calming it down.

David shifted as much as he dared from his safe perch above the beach, and now he could see the back of the cove and a small cave cut into the black rocks. He felt the sensation of being pulled - as if he was looking deeper into the cave. Then he heard the voices - just as last night, rising from the sound of the breaking waves, becoming several voices at once, with the same fear-filled warning:

"*Stay above the sea!*"

He was so upset and confused by the sensation, he failed to notice the boy at first. He appeared outside the cave and stared right at David. On the beach below, he watched Truddi try to restrain the now terrified dog. Then David saw the boy. *Stevie! It had to be!* He saw him clearly, his entire body in view. It appeared to David that he wasn't standing on the sand but floating above it.

David's senses were thrown into confusion as the boy began to float at an obtuse angle up towards David. The boy moved without moving his limbs and this unearthly mode of travelling suddenly brought him directly level with David. David reeled and struggled to remain calm.

"Find me..." the boy said.

"I will Stevie...I promise...where are...?"

But the figure dissolved into nothing, leaving David shaking with emotion like an electrical charge that crackled around his skin.

His feet struggled for grip on a patch of smooth rock, polished by centuries of sea winds and footsteps. He wondered at the colours and patterns of the rock, making it appear as part of a huge snake that was coiled somewhere under the cliffs.

"I can give you what you seek!"

David couldn't prevent his eyes from roaming to the ocean. The sea was speaking to him! It was prepared to give him Stevie back.

"Please. I'll do...whatever."

A sound like distant laughter snapped him from his visions of Stevie being belched up by the sea.

He glanced inland, where movement caught the corner of his eye. Four shapes emerged from a part of the path concealed by a series of thick gorse bushes. They were just children, three of them at least, boys younger than him, dressed in camouflage trousers and tee shirts.

He watched them as they approached, guiding a tall slender girl along the path. She looked out of place with them and as if she didn't want to be there. The smallest boy went past first; his metal water bottle strapped to his belt clinked with each step. He was followed by a taller, chubbier boy, a little older. A shock of ginger hair stuck out from under his baseball cap and framed his sweaty head.

The girl he noticed was much older than he first thought and the boys were very protective of her. She appeared as though she'd had a shock or possibly fainted. She looked at David intensely as she moved closer. The two of them looked at each other without knowing why and he

almost fainted himself when the girl's mouth opened a
fraction and she breathed a whisper:

"David."

She said it as if the name surprised her. And then she
turned away apologetically and staggered on. The third boy
put out a hand to support her and gave a David a severe look
with large, sad blue eyes.

Then they were gone and when he dared to look
behind him he saw only his parents and the Carswells who
appeared on the cliff path above David, making their way
down the tricky path.

David felt as though his blood was ice in his veins. He
struggled to gather his thoughts.

Truddi's Dad helped her with the dog, which, once it
had been taken safely back up to the more level grassland
away from the cliffs, ran off in the direction of a nearby
farmhouse. David was relieved for the dog but had himself
turned pale and quiet once more.

As they walked on again in silence, Truddi spoke in a
confidential tone, ensuring no one else could hear. "It's all
right. It's not your fault you couldn't come down to the
beach. I was okay by myself."

David grunted. She took his pallor to indicate shame
at his lack of courage on the cliffs. He didn't correct her, but
simply increased their walking pace to put distance between
the two of them and the adults. He felt her eyes on him again,
slapping him out of self-absorption. Once or twice his pace
was so fast that it left Truddi panting and she paused once or
twice to catch her breath.

"Wait up!" She called after him.

They all walked together for a while, until they
arrived at a small picnic area. Their parents set about

unpacking lunch. Truddi and David wandered off a little..."to explore".

"...A boy...I saw..." David couldn't get the words out fast enough, unsure at this point what it all meant, what was happening to him. Then Truddi spoke.

"I saw him too." Truddi's words lifted so much weight from him, David almost cried. "I'm sure that's why the dog was barking...dogs can see..." she couldn't say the word 'ghosts'. "But I looked up and saw you talking to this boy...then he just vanished." Truddi offered a hand for David. Finally he took it.

"And I saw someone else on the cliff. A girl. She saw him too, I know she did."

"Did she say anything?" Truddi stood right in front of him, filling his vision.

"Not really. But Stevie said he wanted me to find him. And I can get him back, I know I can."

Truddi turned away to hide her doubtful expression. "Are you sure it's Stevie?"

"Look, I've told you...I should know!"

There was a long silence, during which time David released Truddi's hand and shoved his own securely in his pockets.

Eventually Truddi spoke again. "It's just that...the boy I saw you talking to was wearing funny clothes...old fashioned...Stevie was wearing stuff like that when he died, was he?"

"Come off it! That stuff went out with Queen Victoria!" David realised what he'd just said. Then he added, as much to convince himself as Truddi, "It was Stevie!"

~~~CHAPTER SEVEN~~~

Snared by Your Own Trap

*Why hast thou enticed thyself
Into the old serpent's Paradise?
Why hast thou stolen
Into thyself, thyself?*

Nietzsche

David, grinning and excited, yelled at Stevie. Spluttering the salt water from his mouth he waved his arms around in exhilaration. Now he was as good as his brother. He too could go under the foam and emerge in triumph.

Stevie smiled at his brother's antics. He also smiled with relief. For a second as David had disappeared, he was very anxious. Now he'd seen his brother safe and sound. All was well.

Only then, did Stevie realise he could be in trouble himself. In his concern for his brother, he'd allowed the waves to let him drift too near to the rocks; he was on tip-toe and unbalanced; he hadn't taken a breath and prepared to take on the next wave. All of this flashed through his mind on an instinctive level. But he didn't really have enough time to be totally afraid.

Had the wave washed over him, he'd have been in enough trouble. He was out of his depth. Jagged rocks were looming above the water and he knew only too well about those that lay below the surface.

As it was, the wave began to break immediately behind him. At this point, at the top of its motion, it carried its optimum force. The wave was moving forward quickly;

swelling with the power of tonnes of water; white foaming droplets seemed to hang in the air above the head of water as it positioned itself, like a huge serpent ready to strike.

There was nothing to deflect it from its course. It was heading for the beach where it would burst noisily in a mass of foam and spray. But here was its breaking point. Here it changed from a smooth wall of water to screaming white energy. As it reached Stevie, the power of the breaking wave was like a powerful fist, and it cracked into the back of Stevie's head with bone-splitting force.

David was awake now. He could see himself, staring blankly back, blood oozing from his ears and eyes. How..? He staggered and felt a little faint, but managed to stay upright. His pyjamas were soaked in blood and he realised he was standing at his dressing table; his bloody reflection from the mirror had confused his newly awake senses. Yet how he had come to here was a mystery.

As his senses returned he shivered at the dampness of the blood saturating his pyjamas. Bringing himself to look into the mirror through misty eyes he could see the blood running from his eyes and down the sides of his face. His hair was wet and matted. His hands trembled and his mind heard the continual clap of the wave hitting Stevie on the back of the head, shattering his skull, snapping his neck. He heard it. He *felt* it.

Then he tugged himself away from his reflection. The wind was blowing through his window, slapping the plastic blind-pull onto the window frame with a loud clap. *There's always a logical answer!*

The blood looked worse than it was; a nose bleed that had gone unchecked as he slept and bled into his eyes and ears. His mother cleaned him up and rationalised everything. He accepted her reasoning...but she still couldn't explain away the pain in the back of his head.

His mother fussed and nursed him throughout the morning. It was the same relationship they'd had for years now. She wasn't going to risk losing another son, not even to a germ. Over the years the strain on her face had changed, from the look of a mother who had lost a son, to the look of a mother who was afraid to lose another one.

David had been happy to play the role she had written for him. At home he would be content to be wrapped in a blanket on the sofa at the first sign of a cold or a bump on the knee. He could have time off school or avoid family gatherings with his grotesque aunts and drunken uncles; because he knew his mother would be sympathetic to his needs.

As she fussed around him on the bed, ensuring that no lasting damage had been done following his nose bleed, he saw Truddi standing in the doorway. For the first time he sensed that his behaviour and his use of his mother as a nurse wasn't quite right. He saw it in Truddi's eyes and he began to feel uncomfortable. Yet all the same, when he told his mother firmly that he was all right and wanted to go out, his mother appeared greatly offended.

He and Truddi spent the day in the town, wasting money on novelties and junk food. It was a good while before the ache in the back of his head finally subsided. It was as if he had felt the force of the wave that hit Stevie and his own skull had been broken. Yet something else was bothering him too.

His dreams had always been the same. First he was himself, then he was Stevie, then he drowned. However, since they'd come back to Cornwall, there was something else about the dreams. He would need to think more about it, before he spoke to Truddi. One thing was definite; this new feeling was stronger in the dream last night: the feeling that there had been something else in the water with Stevie. Something dangerous. Something old and powerful.

Something *hungry.*

~ ~ ~ ~

It had become normal from about six-thirty for the two families to spend an eternity dressing for dinner. Tonight they were all going to drive to a neighbouring village, Morullion, to a pub where guest bands played outside until late.

David, as usual, had been ready for ages; his appearance wasn't something he spent too much time on. The parents were still rushing back and forth, trying on this and that. Truddi appeared in David's room. Not for the first time, David noticed how very pretty she was. Her deep brown hair shone in the light and her dress had thin shoulder straps, which revealed her neck and broad shoulders. David struggled to conceal his reaction which obviously made her feel complimented and for a while as they talked, he couldn't stop looking at her.

Truddi browsed through the books on the shelf in David's room. Old books, some more read than others.

"I wonder how many people have looked at these books before us." She spoke almost to herself. "The Bible, Huckleberry Finn, Moominland Midwinter. Do you like books, David?"

"I don't mind."

"And who are the people that read these books? Do you think anyone famous has stayed here?"

"Who knows!" or *'Who cares?'* David was just happy to talk to her.

"That's the thing about books. A hundred people could read the same book...this one..." she pulled out a tatty volume and flicked the pages over. "And they all might...see it differently."

She replaced the book with a guide book to the Lizard Peninsula, complete with maps. She picked it up and opened it out on the bed.

"So Stevie disappeared here, you say?" She pointed to a place on the map.

"Yes...that's where we stayed on holiday." He pointed to the place name on the map that was carved into his memory, into his very soul. *Porthminion!*

"But...it just seems unlikely that his ghost should have travelled all this way around the coast to end up here...it just doesn't make sense..."

"Stop it! Why won't you believe me? It's Stevie and he needs me!"

He watched as Truddi re-folded the map in silence. *Why does she want to hurt me? Doesn't she realise?*

Truddi fixed him with a stern stare. "Do you have any photos of Stevie?"

David sighed, but in the short time he'd known her, he'd found out that she was a fighter. She was persistent and she was going to pursue this argument until she was satisfied.

"My Mum always carries one in her bag."

~ ~ ~ ~

Truddi crept into Mr and Mrs Givens' room. Mrs Givens could be heard in the adjoining bathroom. Truddi quickly found the bag and opened it. She took a deep breath before diving in. Invading other people's rooms was bad enough, but a woman's private bag? She felt a pang of conscience but quickly found what she wanted. If Mrs Givens startled her, she regained her composure swiftly.

"Truddi? Can I help you?"

"Yes thanks...you look nice!" *Masterful, Truddi!*

"Do I? Do you think so? I'm not sure...the dress I like, but...which shoes?"

"The pale ones...most definitely. And this purse...er...bag." *Even better Truddi!*

"Yes...I think so too. Thanks Truddi...it's nice to have another female's opinion of fashion...living with men has its drawbacks."

"That's okay." She made to leave.

"And I think you look smashing Truddi, you really do." Truddi nodded and glided out of the room, then once through the door she pulled her dress up over her knees and ran across the landing to David's room.

So what if he hates me for it? He doesn't realise what people are doing for him. Anyway, he may hate me, but he'll see I'm right and he'll forgive me.

She burst into the room and stood face to face with David.

"This isn't the boy I saw with you on the beach!" Stevie's picture was thrust in David's face, demanding he look at it. Truddi had confronted him with this, now she had to stand back and let the fireworks start. "Tell me why Stevie should be different! Have a different face and wearing old clothes. He doesn't look like Stevie, because he's not Stevie! The ghost you've been seeing isn't your brother!"

~~~CHAPTER EIGHT~~~

The Lizard Amulet

Vishnu sleeps on the coils of the serpent Shesha (Duration) who is also called Ananta (Endless) on whose hoods rests the earth. This serpent or naga king serves also as the bracelet of Lord Shiva and can function as his bowstring or his chariot axle. The serpent is the primordial sustainer who holds up the earth on his head. Every now and then, he must shift his position, relax his head and neck and thereby he is the cause of earthquakes.

David and Truddi didn't speak to each other right through the meal. Their parents weren't slow to notice this. Despite David's dad making hopeless attempts to involve them both in conversation, they sat in silence apart from mono-syllable replies to direct questions.

As it began to get dark outside, the garden and car park were lit up with coloured lights. The three piece band had completed their sound checks and began playing to a sizeable crowd of locals and holiday makers. The heavy bass reverberated through the old pub. Truddi had been fidgeting all night, waiting to hear some British music. With a nod of approval from her dad, she trotted outside. That David didn't follow her, merely confirmed the tiff to the adults.

Mrs Givens, however, could be as provocative as Truddi. "Truddi looks lovely tonight, don't you think David?" David grunted and looked away.

Mr Givens craned his neck to see out of the window into the garden. "Who's that boy she's talking to?"

David said nothing and pretended to read the beer mat again, and then he asked if he could go out to see the band. Mr Givens watched him go and winked at his grinning wife.

David made his way through the throng that filled the car park and over to the small garden at the rear of the pub. When he saw her she was alone. Her hair shone black-red under the lights and she seemed as if she was in a trance, her gaze locked on to the performers. She swayed gently although the music pounded. He knew when he looked at her at that moment, she was special.

Another boy had obviously had the same feelings. He walked over to her and handed her a glass of Cola. She smiled to thank him and they began talking, nodding in appreciation of the band. She laughed, too often for David's liking. He had to think quickly.

"Oh there you are, Truddi. Your Mum wants a word with you." Truddi smiled apologetically at the boy and followed David. Once out of harm's way, he turned. "I lied. I need to speak to you."

"What about, David?"

"Ghosts..?" He sounded feeble.

"Whose?"

"Ours? I mean..." David's worst fears were coming true. She had grown tired of his ghosts and apparitions. He was losing her. "I don't understand...it ought to be Stevie. Don't you think?"

"I don't understand either, David. But we'll work it out." She smiled at him. Perhaps things were all right then. "Why did you come outside? That boy was being nice to me."

"To stop you...to apologize. I know you were only trying to help."

The song ended and applause rang out around the car park and beer garden. This band was popular. They were jostled as a group of newcomers pushed their way nearer to the stage.

For a moment they were separated and Truddi found herself looking around for him.

He deliberately stepped in to get me away from that boy! She thought. She could see David fighting his way through the squeeze of bodies to reach her again. She fought back a chuckle as he took more than three bad bumps on his face from elbows and shoulders and he looked so out of place in a crowd. As if he was drowning...

Truddi didn't even pretend to be annoyed with him. He'd come around sooner than she'd expected after her aggressive display at the hotel. *He respects my opinions, she thought.*

"David?" He stopped checking his face for bruises and looked at her. "Tonight, can we not talk about ghosts, coffins, whatever-it-is-man or anything else of that sort? We're on holiday. Let's be more...carefree!"

She offered him some Cola and he did his best to appear happy. They elbowed themselves to a good spot at the side of the stage and although David's face announced to everyone he'd have sooner been anywhere else, except perhaps the beach, Truddi felt the weight lift from her shoulders as she lost herself in the music.

Truddi liked the band. The girl singer's haunting vocals layered over synthesizer bass and drums buried themselves deep into Truddi's psyche. The words of one of the songs seemed to have more relevance to her than the rest:

"Summer spies in my room
Disturbed eyes look over you
Secrets, our movements seen
Despair, a shadow turns to blue"

The night stayed warm and the two of them spent the whole evening under the coloured lights of the beer garden. They applauded loudly each time a song ended, and before long the band members began to smile at them and appreciate the good musical taste of their newest fans.

Truddi knew David was only feigning appreciation of the band to please her, but no matter. Tonight he would have to take second seat to her needs; tonight it was about her instead.

The music, floating notes over pounding beats, seemed to hold Truddi captive. This was different to the sort of music she was used to in Australia. There was something new about it, untamed. She wasn't a big lover of the sort of pop music her friends were in to, but this music...involved her.

As the area around the pub melted into darkness, everything seemed to focus on the small stage area, tucked into the car park, lit by a few bright lights, un-changing and stark. The softer coloured bulbs around the garden blurred in her vision as all attention remained on the band...on the female singer especially.

"They're really good aren't they?" she eventually turned back to David between numbers.

"Yeah...I suppose..." David smiled nervously at Truddi. This was the fourth time she'd asked him the same question. He wasn't as enthusiastic about them as her, in fact, she thought, *I bet he hates them really. He's only saying they're good because I like them. Oh well, it's a start!*

A small insect blew onto her face on the breath of the evening breeze. He had an excuse to touch her face and didn't hesitate. She smiled and then looked back to the band as they started a new number.

She thought for a moment about David. Music didn't seem to stir him at all. It occurred to her that she knew little about his interests. *He has no interests!* She thought. *The sea is certainly a non-starter, but it's as if his whole life is an avoidance of anything that would remind him of his brother. How many songs or poems were written about the sea? How much music is evocative of an ocean? The only things he ever talks about are his ghosts and how troubled he is!*

For a moment she thought of Den Genero, her old boyfriend in Cairns. *Den Genero! What a self-centred, egotistical, up his own..!* She remembered how he always compared her to other girls he'd been with. *Do I go for boys who are self-obsessed? Is that my 'type'?*

She found herself staring at the singer again, whose eyes closed as she twined herself around the microphone stand. Her face was so full of expression. Every word, every note was a feeling despatched through the amplifier:

> *"Walking in silence,*
> *Run away, in silence,*
> *Your confusion, your shield,*
> *My mask of illusion*
> *My self hate,*
> *My wall of fears,*
> *Don't walk away..."*

As Truddi watched and listened, something strange happened. She could see the singer, her eyes closed; breathing wistful feminine notes over the heavy bass and drums. Yet, as she watched, the girl's eyes opened suddenly, staring right into hers. And although Truddi could see the singer's lips mouth the words of the song, all she heard was another voice, deeper, much deeper. A voice that was inhuman and had a sensation with it that seemed to carry the coldness and darkness from the bowels of the earth. She felt her insides lose all warmth and the power of the voice growled into her, filling every cell with its message, a message that she gave words to:

"You'll die if you return, girl!"

She felt the air leave her body and she gasped to breathe in fresh, warm summer night air to stem the chill in her veins. When she looked at the singer again she was as before, singing her song to the faceless crowd. She felt David grab her arm and pull her to a wooden bench.

"You okay, Truddi?"

"I...I don't..." Truddi tried to gather herself; she didn't like being caught off guard like that. Her mind raced to explain what had just happened. David, she could tell, had been oblivious to any 'voice'. And she wasn't too keen on the death threat, which was so obviously meant for her. She mumbled about being fine and was about to get up when she saw the singer walking towards her.

"Hey...are you okay?" the singer asked, with genuine concern on her face.

Truddi warmed to her immediately. This girl wasn't to blame for the 'message' she'd received, that was clear. "Sure...much better now..."

The singer smiled bigger than ever. "You're an Aussie! Great." She sat down beside Truddi. "You're sure you're okay? Only...we've all got used to hearing you cheer for us at the end of each song, it's been great." She leant closer to Truddi and spoke in a confidential tone. "It encourages the rest of them to clap, too. British audiences are so stand-offish, you know what I mean?"

Truddi smiled and thought of David then nodded. She liked the girl even better now she was closer. She had a friendly face, more than a little bit familiar. She didn't bother to give the girl the true nature of her nationality. It was too complicated. Besides she was used to it, her Australian accent was going to stay with her for a while longer yet.

"I just came over a bit...faint...nothing serious..."

"Hey...I know...I've been there. Perhaps you're hungry..."

"No...I'm fine now, thanks. I just had a funny feeling, as if...as if I shouldn't ever come back to England again." Truddi didn't know why she said it. It was stupid to say it. None of it made sense. She hadn't given any thought to coming back to England anyway.

David caught her eye briefly and gave her a quizzical look. The singer however didn't think it strange at all. Her eyebrows tightened with concern and she held Truddi's hand, tightly, and Truddi felt the last of the cold leave her, to be replaced by a warmth that flowed from her hand around the rest of her body.

"No...You'll be with us again. One day. Here..." she pressed a metal object into Truddi's palm, "...a souvenir of the Lizard and remember...some keys open two doors." With that she left and walked back to the stage.

Truddi opened her palm to see a small charm for a bracelet, in the shape of a key with a Lizard's head at one end. The rest of the key was the Lizard's body and the teeth of the key were its tail. 'Two doors?' repeated Truddi to herself.

"What was all that about?" asked a confused David.

"I guess she's just trying to be nice," Truddi put the whole thing to the back of her mind as best she could and continued to enjoy the rest of the night.

Soon it was time to head back to the hotel. She had wanted to talk to the singer but the band had been swallowed up after their gig by roadies, groupies and too many people not really going anywhere. She clutched the charm tightly as they walked the winding streets back to the hotel.

Truddi had never had problems sleeping. When you're active, the body seems to revel in good, deep slumber. She never had any sleep disorders and she wasn't a nervous type. So when she woke suddenly, with a feeling of intense cold right through to her bones, it took her a moment to recover from the initial shock. She could see her own face, pale and frightened, floating before her.

Whilst terrible explanations raced around her still waking mind, she discovered that she was sitting at her dressing table, and it was her reflection in the mirror that she saw. But what was she doing there?

Then she noticed her right arm, reaching straight out towards the mirror. She saw it, but she had no feeling in it. It wasn't under her control. For the first time she noticed something other than her face in the mirror. In her hand was the deep red lipstick she'd worn that night, and her hand was writing on the mirror with it, the red letters like a veil in front of her horrified reflection.

S t E u i

Her scream was hardly audible, but it seemed to eject whatever had been controlling her from her body. Her head jerked backwards and her right arm crashed limply onto the dressing table.

Stevie? The name flashed into her mind. Then she heard another scream. Louder than hers had been, and this was a boy's scream, a boy in sheer terror.

When Truddi heard the scream, she set about wiping the lipstick letters from the mirror with a moist tissue.

~~~~

David too had been woken. He ought to have slept well that night. He did fall asleep as soon as he hit the bed, but it was a nervous sleep. His subconscious mind embroidered a tortured quilt of images that covered his sleeping body. To hide from terrifying thoughts he pulled the quilt over his head, but this only sent him further down where the patchwork was of darker images. He woke often and listened for whispered voices. Perhaps Truddi's denial that the ghostly visitor was Stevie had sent his brother away - had he deserted his beloved Stevie again?

He lay on his back, sensing something, but he wasn't sure what. He began to struggle for breath as if he were drowning and he lay still, helpless as his duvet seemed to be pulled from the bottom of the bed. In breathless horror, he watched it slip past his knees and he felt the sensation of pressure increasing all over him, pinning him down. He watched the duvet uncover his legs and his eyes widened in terror. Across his bare legs he saw a wriggling, seething, hissing mass of worms, piled high, eating into his flesh. He was unable to move, to kick them away. All that was left was to scream.

Mr and Mrs Givens found David in his uncovered bed. The worms weren't real, but the accident in his bed was. *No one else must know about this!* He begged for the world to shut them off, to isolate them from the rest of the hotel. *The other guests pretend to be trying to help, to be concerned, to show well-meaning. But they're just being nosey! Don't let them see what I've done, please!*

His mother fussed around him but he was already wishing he could've handled this by himself. His boxer shorts and the sheet below were wet. Mr Givens had to turn away for a moment. He helped his wife remove the sheet and they carried it out of the room and made for the laundry.

"What sort of 'demons' can give a teenage boy such nightmares and make him wet the bed?" Mr Givens' voice carried down the landing.

"Don't be angry, it's not his fault..." Mrs Givens tried to placate her husband.

"I'm not angry with David. I'm angry at Doctor Campbell. And myself for listening to all the 'experts'! This holiday is a bad idea!"

"It has to work..."

Back in his room David was distraught. He had spent years perfecting the art of dividing his parents, getting them to argue, question themselves. Listening to them quarrel as they made their way across the landing was not what he wanted. He'd had enough of the wedge he'd driven between them. He needed them to be stronger for him now. And he'd spent the last nine years weakening them both.

~ ~ ~CHAPTER NINE~ ~ ~

The Dragon's Lair

*"Be ye therefore wise as serpents,
and harmless as doves."*

Matthew; 10:16

The cliff walk the next day took the two families along the coast in the opposite direction to their normal route. Again, Truddi and David 'explored' ahead. The parents were in solemn mood. David's behaviour was becoming a concern for them all. At first he'd shown signs of improvement, but the improvement had been short-lived. In some ways things were much worse.

The weather had cleared completely and the path brought them to a tiny village tucked into a rocky cove. There they sat at a small tearoom and ignoring the health warnings, set about ridding the world of six deadly cream teas.

"You seem quiet!" Mr Givens showed great perception and it was clear to Truddi he noticed she and David had not been their usual chatty selves. Truddi thought that Mr Givens assumed there were still leftover issues from meal time at the pub last night.

Truddi knew he was miles from the truth. She was more perceptive than him. She could tell David had something to tell her about last night, and she knew that she also had a bombshell for David. She knew how David thought, and what he was thinking, because in this situation it was the same as her.

The clotted cream and scones were not the sole reason for their silence. Both of them also had something they didn't want the other to know about last night. Both were scared that in their normal excitable chatter, they'd give the game away.

The two of them sat at their own table, out of earshot from their parents.

"So...do you ever think you'll stop being scared of the sea?" The question seemed to come from nowhere. Truddi didn't appear to be desperate for a response. She'd developed a taste for weak, sweet tea and poured herself another cup.

"Maybe, someday."

"Why not today then?" seemed a fair question but she could tell from his expression as she stirred her tea loudly, that David thought it wasn't fair.

"Why? Because the last time I saw the sea, it swallowed my brother!"

Oh come on! Thought Truddi. *Do you want me to cry? Get tough, boy.* "But...you said you might be able to go back to the sea...one day...so there's going to be a day when you won't be scared of it...one day, so why spend any more time being scared now? Just do it now, have that day now and get back to living...without fear."

"I said 'maybe'!"

"You don't want to go and sit on the beach? Play in the sand? Play football? Sun bathe?"

"No!"

"What happens if that's what I want to do?"

"I won't come with you!"

After the scones and clotted cream had been demolished, it was time to continue the walk. The two sets of parents never stopped talking although David and Truddi always kept a good distance away from them. Truddi had noticed more than once that she and David were under fierce parental scrutiny.

They walked on a little further. The silence between her and David was becoming intolerable, a wall, higher and higher with every passing minute. Truddi felt it. They could go on, shutting each other out. It would only end one way; the end of their friendship.

Back in Cairns, Truddi had a reputation for no-nonsense talk. She could be stubborn and uncompromising. Yet she knew now that to save this friendship - if she wanted to - she would have to give some ground.

Do I want to save the friendship? She looked at him. *Until a week or so I didn't know you. You're English. There won't be much of a friendship when I go to Canada. You're younger than me. You sulk. You're sulking now! I hate sulking. You're troubled - deeply. You hate the sea.*

You need me. I can help. If you let me. We're on an adventure - with real dead ghosts!

And I need you. I like you!

"Last night...I...something got inside me...made me write something on my mirror with lipstick...I wrote...Stevie!"

David turned to face her. "I don't know what to say..." His mouth opened a few times but nothing came out. Yes! She thought. *You have realised the enormity of what I have said. Thank you!*

"Whatever has been targeting me...from beyond the grave, has switched its attention to you." He stumbled verbally. "We're sharing the burden. Is that it?"

"Looks like we're in it together!" She fixed him with her eyes and saw the relief sweep over him, making him choke back the tears. He could do nothing but place a hand on each of her shoulders and pull himself towards her.

They hugged in silence then she told him all about it. The way her arm had been numb, moving as if it wasn't hers. The way she'd woken up sitting at the dressing table. The name Stevie, clearly there for all to see.

He replied by telling her about his ordeal with the worms - but avoided telling her how the horror had affected him as he was too ashamed.

Once the air had been cleared, they began to relax once more into holiday mood.

As they ran ahead of their parents, at full pelt down the grassy slopes, no one could've guessed the traumas that plagued them both. Whilst running they could see the cliff edge, far off ahead of them and they kept it in mind as they gathered pace down the slope. Both were mindful that when hurtling down a slope of slippery grass, sudden stops are difficult.

Yet that's precisely what happened. David couldn't stop quickly enough and was already skidding out of control as he tried to slam on the brakes. Truddi's iron grip on his arm was the anchor that prevented David from falling from a premature precipice.

"Where did that come from?" David gasped and held Truddi's arm until he caught his breath. Hidden by long grass, a huge crater had almost swallowed them both up.

They both gathered their senses. Their hearts were beating fast at the narrow escape. "I wonder how many people *that* has caught out!" David even managed a nervous looking smile.

They walked closer, carefully. Some cataclysmic act had created a huge hole, almost a perfect circle; its sides were sheer but now covered in grass most of the way down the fifty metre drop. A small opening remained at the bottom to let sea water fizz through and around the fallen rocks that were the floor of this pit.

They came across a small sign on a wooden stake near the unguarded edge of the hole:

> "The Dragon's Lair. On September 14th 1847,
> following a terrible storm, high seas caused the
> collapse of a large cave in the cliffs. The softer
> rocks around the sides and roof collapsed.
> The crater was named by locals,
> 'The Dragon's Lair'".

"The sea did this?" Truddi almost gasped.

"It is capable of terrible things, you know." David flashed a momentary dark mood, but the warm sun and gentle breeze were filling two troubled young souls with lighter holiday feelings.

Truddi managed to guide David to a rocky viewpoint at the top of the cliff. The sea was on three sides of them, but a long way below. David lay flat on the rocks and for the first time, he found some enjoyment in looking across the coastline, perhaps because at this distance, the blue sea appeared flat, two dimensional, safe. A child's thick poster paint brushwork on the landscape. Not the real sea.

"You want to know what I think?" Truddi flipped herself onto her back and ran her fingers through her hair. She enjoyed the feeling of the sun on her face and the salt drifted through the air coating her lips. She missed the sea.

There was no reply and she opened her eyes and gave David a sideways glance from behind her hair. He was looking at her, the way boys often looked at her.

"What are you looking at?" She faked a voice of threat and menace which she hoped wouldn't destroy any courage he had.

"The curl of your eyelashes when your eyes are shut."

Truddi almost choked. *What? Are you really saying that to me?* She exhaled her surprise. "Yeah?"

"And those dainty ear studs, just nestled on your earlobes."

"David? Are you kidding me?" She sat up on her elbows and looked at him. He had a look that reminded her of Vince Carson when he was about to do the half-pipe at the board park for the first time. The task ahead was terrifying but if he gritted his teeth he may just about do it. She wondered if David had the strength to go on. And did she want him to?

"I'm looking at your skin. It's a sunny, gold colour. Not like my skin, not like anyone's in this country, ours are pale, almost transparent."

"David..." Her words broke the spell and he averted his eyes.

"You asked me what I was looking at. I'm hardly likely to look at the sea, am I?"

She knew he was covering his true feelings. But that was all right. If he'd continued in the same way it all might have turned awkward. She rolled back onto her side and rested her head on her arm. She gave him a warm smile and continued.

"I'll tell you what I think anyway! I had a friend in Queensland. Jessica. She had Aboriginal blood in her somewhere down the line. She told me the strangest thing once." For a moment, Truddi remembered Jessica and how she was already missing her so much. She thought of her round jolly face and big eyes. Perhaps only now did it sink in that she would probably never see her again.

"She told me about her Aboriginal ancestors, and the way they hunted. One hunter would make it obvious he was there, the quarry would see him and move cautiously, but stay focussed on him, waiting for him to attack. And all the while, a second hunter would be creeping up on them from the other side."

David raised his eyebrows. "Yes, I can see the relevance. That's exactly what's happening here!"

Truddi smiled. "I don't know what made me think of it, but the way Jessica told me, the week before I left, she was so serious, it was so unlike her."

Truddi could see that David was still not sure what she was getting at. "I'm thinking," she said slowly, carefully, "that there's two things going on here. Two *different* things. One more dangerous than the other. One of them a decoy!"

Truddi heard again the threats and mockery of the Serpent. *'He comes to me willingly.'* For the first time as her thoughts raced she made a connection. She gave David a quick glance, which was enough to convince her he wasn't possessed. *Still, there's a good chance he's being used!*

She expected David to fly off in a mood, not even willing to consider that he and his problems were not at the centre of everything. Instead he nodded. "You may be right."

"The ghost stuff is bad enough, and we're right to spend time on it. But we've been distracted!" Truddi stood up and David rose to his feet and waited for her to finish. "But I think we need to find out about the ghoul at the hotel and his coffin. That's what we should be paying attention to!" *Steer David away from his absorption with Stevie.*

The air filled with seagulls and their cries heralded a distant roll of thunder. She straightened her clothes and threw David a warm smile which bounced back to her immediately. She told herself how clever she had been. Her task was to break David out of his obsession, his quest to bring Stevie back from the dead. The Serpent was simply a manifestation of the dark path he was taking, *willingly.*

It was a rational world. And there was her answer.

"You cannot resist me!"

She turned quickly, to see David with a huge grin on his face.

"What did you say?" Her voice quivering and her features a depiction of vanishing composure.

"I said: you can't resist me..." David's smile faded. He gestured wildly at her exposed shoulder. "You...you look like you're trying to...attract my attention..." He wilted before her eyes and turned his back on her but his blushes radiated out through his ears.

Truddi took a moment to realise that her loose summer top had slipped from a shoulder revealing her bra strap. She wanted to smile, the relief twitched at the corners of her mouth. *It's a rational world!* She pulled her top back into position.

"I was only joking...it struck me as funny..." David fumbled around his excuses and she felt sorry for him. It wasn't his fault. Still, she was struggling to form words through her clenched teeth.

"I know...so was I."

~~~CHAPTER TEN~~~

Misdirection

Satan; who, in the serpent, hath contrived
Against us this deceit: to crush his head
Would be revenge indeed!

Paradise Lost, Book X, Milton

The clock in the hall of the Prince Albert Hotel struck twelve. Some new guests had arrived during the day and they were the type who liked to stay up late in the bar. Mrs Kirkman glanced up from serving them more drink and gave an anxious look to the clock in the hall.

The light from the bar illuminated the clock face that stood in the otherwise dark hall. Through the candlewick rails of the banister, David and Truddi pressed their faces, straining to hear the tell tale sounds they were waiting for.

The sound of wood scraping on stone somewhere in the hotel gave them their cue and they crept down the stairs to the hall.

Truddi pressed herself against the wall and darted a quick look into the kitchen. "He's there! Look!"

"The coffin! Oh I didn't want to see that..!" David drooped.

They remained silent, motionless and watched the ghoul pull his cargo from the service lift and drag it towards the kitchen through the breakfast room. Before they could rise or say anything, a cold breath seemed to pass right through them.

They both turned and looked up the dark stairs. White grey wisps of cold vapours swam into each other, spiralling and increasing in speed and density as they pulled together. Before their eyes, the shape of the boy - their boy - materialised. He floated silently and through him and around him was a pale, silver light that smeared his features.

"Help me...please."

The vision seemed to fade quickly, as if his strength was fading. David and Truddi winced at a foul smell of rotting fish and seaweed. Between themselves and the boy a film of water appeared, floating horizontally at waist level. It was almost two dimensional. It had length and width, but it appeared no thicker than a sheet of paper.

It shimmered as if it were water catching the moonlight. The boy wrote in it. The two children watched as the water parted for his finger, tracing the path before becoming smooth water once more. The letters he traced fading before he could end the word he wrote:

$$S \quad t \quad \mathcal{E} \quad u \quad i$$

The water screen flipped vertically upwards, making a narrow wall; the boy on one side, David and Truddi on the other. The water concealed the boy completely. Then it began to foam and swirl like a great whirlpool. It moved backwards and enveloped the boy who spluttered briefly before he and all traces of water were gone.

Truddi glanced into the kitchen but by now the ghoul had gone. Her eyes narrowed with defiance. *A decoy!* She thought. "We won't be following the whatever-it-is-man tonight!"

David nodded but his face told her he wasn't sorry.

"I know what you said, Truddi. It all makes sense. But...I still feel as though the boy is tugging at me. He's the cause of my nightmares. He's the one linked to Stevie somehow..."

Truddi was about to speak when a door opened off the hall, casting light into the hall. Holding their breaths they pressed themselves into the shadows and the side of the clock. A figure entered and stood for a moment, caught in the half light. It was Mr Kirkman. He fumbled with a bunch of keys and then joined the others in the bar.

Truddi grabbed David by the hand and led him upstairs to her room. Her mind was racing. She flicked on the kettle.

"David...whenever you've seen the ghost words...think now, you say it read 'Stevie'. Did it actually write the whole word 'Stevie'?"

"Well no, just like now, something always stopped it from completing the last 'e'."

Truddi sat down on the bed next to him. "I hadn't thought of it before...just like you...I presumed that when I jolted out of my trance at the mirror, writing with lipstick, that I prevented the last 'e' from being written, because with me, there was just this red line that dragged all the way down the mirror as my arm fell."

"And...?"

"There was a similar line just now...when that boy wrote in the water. What if there isn't supposed to be a last 'e'? What if it's another letter?"

"I don't get it!"

Truddi pressed the point. "David. I know you don't want to believe it, I know it's important that somehow this keeps your brother in there somewhere, but I really think... he's not!"

"So..." gulped David, "Just a line? Another 'i'? Stevii? Is that what you're saying? Is that a foreign name?" David barked out his disgust. "It was just an unfinished 'e', that's all!"

"How about an 'l'?" said Truddi.

"*Stevil?* That's even worse!"

Truddi was formulating ideas just ahead of speaking them. But as she progressed she was more convinced of their correctness. "No...On the mirror...and just now on the water...the 'e' was a capital 'E'."

David stroked his chin to help him remember. "Yeah...same with me...I think..."

"So..." Truddi had gone this far with the supposition; she needed David to find the answer too. "It's a capital 'E'!"

"So what does..?" David wasn't thinking as fast as Truddi.

"It's two words, David. Not 'Stevie' or 'Stevil'...it's 'St. Evil'!"

The word brought with it a new fear. Through all the boy's ghostly antics, he'd never appeared hostile. Now Evil had come out to play, all good children should run away. As David repeated the new found words over and over, Truddi made them some instant hot chocolate from the tray provided by the hotel on her bedside table.

"I don't even remember a Saint Evil. It can't be right. They wouldn't have made someone a saint with Evil for a name!" David looked desperate, trying to find a way back to Stevie. They bounced half ideas around for a while, speaking without thinking in the hope that one of their solutions may prove to be right.

Truddi handed David a mug of hot chocolate. "Do you think we'd better tell someone now? I just feel that we've suddenly gone right out of our depth."

"*St. Evil?*"

"I'm scared, David!"

"You're scared?" David grinned. "Me too. Although, in a crazy way, this whole thing has become less frightening and more interesting!"

~~~CHAPTER ELEVEN~~~

Until La Luain

*When Saint Patrick rid Ireland of snakes, one serpent
was allowed to remain. A giant water serpent, now
called the Lough Derg Monster was tricked by Patrick
to stay at the bottom of Lough Derg until La Luain,
which the snake understood to be Monday, but can
also mean the Apocalyptic Last Day.
So the snake is confined for ever
and a day to the lake.*

It was another day of clotted cream teas and gentle
exercise. Their parents had decided to visit a town that
evening, with a small harbour and a large bandstand in a
hillside park. David and Truddi made every effort to
accommodate their parent's desire to listen to the local brass
band playing Andrew Lloyd Webber medleys, but they
managed to persuade the 'oldies' to let them spend some
money in the seaside shops and amusements.

There were many young people around that town,
the water sports of Cornwall's coastline attracted teenagers
from far and wide. They spent a lot of money on some hi-tech
video games, and then treated themselves to a candy floss
each. The moment Truddi saw the poster in the shop window
she was torn.

More than an hour later, the poster still tugged at her.
A surfing competition, open to all, was taking place in this
town tomorrow. This was what she needed, more than she
had thought possible.

"You do realise," she said casually, "that I've come all the way over here from Australia and this is the first taste of the British seaside I've really had?"

David wasn't much bothered.

"The little shops, harbours, a real English resort. I've only ever seen the sea from cliff tops, or tiny rocky coves and had to escape from them as soon as possible." She was prepared to discount the few early mornings she'd taken herself surfing at some damp, grey cove.

David remained unmoved.

"So...how about spending a day on a beach..."

"No way!" The interruption was swift and blunt.

"You wouldn't have to go in the sea. Just sit at the back of the beach. It'd be nice."

"You know I can't..."

He thinks that's the end of it! She thought. *He doesn't understand, he can't understand how much I need this.*

"You know, surfing is important to me."

"I know. But I can't go..."

"I left my friends behind, all the things I used to do, my whole life. We are going to have a nice house on the beach in Canada, but I know the sea there is no good for surfing." She wanted him to enthuse about her surfing, even if it meant nothing to him.

"You want me to be sick?" He gave her a look of finality.

David had grown used to having his own way over anything. His mum would acquiesce at the drop of a hat. Even Truddi had bent over backwards for him. She prepared to concede once more.

As the daylight faded to be replaced by hundreds of coloured bulbs hung across the streets, they walked and chatted amongst a growing number of revellers.

Life! Truddi felt herself smiling; at the people, the laughter, the vibrancy of the seaside town that had come to colourful life on the summer evening. She smiled because this was what she'd thought England would be like.

She was tired of being surrounded by death and danger. The only thing good about that was the friendship that was growing between her and David. And then she smiled because she had a plan to do what she loved to do and it wouldn't make David feel 'sick'. She smiled because of the boy at her side and began to feel that he was special to her.

She thought of making trips back to England in years to come. And as she thought that, for a split second a pair of red eyes snarled at her menacingly, thrusting into her face. Her step faltered briefly and the eyes faded as quickly as they had come, leaving her staring at the flashing sign of two red neon lights outside the amusements, and she gathered herself together.

"You all right?" asked David. Truddi nodded and they walked on.

~~~~

David awoke next morning and realised he'd slept right through the night. No ghostly visits, no nightmares. In a strange way, he'd missed the ghostly boy. But there was another peculiar feel to the morning. The absence of something else.

Mr Givens proudly displayed his abilities with the mouth trumpet and he performed a repeat of last night's brass band medley all through breakfast.

As David dived in to his usual hearty breakfast, he began to fidget impatiently. The Carswells' table was still empty. He checked his watch. Each time the door opened he looked up expecting to see Truddi and her parents walk in. He finished his bacon, eggs and mushrooms. Still no sign of them.

"I'll go and find Truddi," he said, gulping down the last of his fourth cup of tea.

"She's not here," said his mother, almost off hand.

"Where...?"

"Her parents wanted to go somewhere today - as we do," said Dad, flatly.

"But..."

"You can't expect them to come all the way over here and spend every waking moment with us!" His mother's words smacked of a parental conspiracy.

What else was going on? If they had to go somewhere else, why had they gone so early? Why hadn't Truddi said anything?

David spent the entire car ride in a miserable silence. His parents had decided to travel further inland and visit a former silver mine. *This was going to be so thrilling! Not!!* He couldn't get Truddi out of his mind. When she wasn't at his side it was like losing...a sibling!

The car ride was over-long and for the first time this holiday David found himself wanting to be near the sea...anywhere, so long as it was near Truddi.

The old mine had been turned into a sort of leisure park, with boating lakes and mini golf courses built around the remaining buildings; former engine houses now renovated to become focal points in the amusement park. These buildings were designed now for the total amusement of tourists. David wondered at the lack of respect for the people that used to work here, but only briefly as he began to enjoy himself. The tall chimneys, once sentinels for the mine shafts, stood now like giant parents watching over scores of playful children.

David and his parents followed the exhibition trail around the park, but David couldn't bring himself to be interested in the displays and boards telling the history of the mine.

In the North Wheal engine house, where a Guide was telling a small group of tourists about the building, David noticed a small boy handing out chocolates from a wooden tray strung around his neck. In keeping with the 'theme park' way, he was dressed in period costume. David looked at him and noticed the collarless shirt and rough trousers that had recently become only too familiar to him.

The same type of clothes 'our' boy wears! David gritted his teeth. *Our boy?* He held his thoughts for a moment. For the first time he was preparing to admit that his ghostly visitor was not his brother.

The Guide's words also jolted him from his wonderings. He mentioned a storm in 1847 and a mining disaster. David's parents left to continue the walk, but David stayed behind and begged the Guide to go into further detail.

He was old, sort of Granddad's age, and David wondered if the Guide had family involvement in the story he was telling. Perhaps the old man's Grandparents had been there. For whatever reason, the Guide spoke with knowledge and feeling and told the story that had impacted on his home village so dramatically.

"It was September 1847. The weather had been dry for a long time, but then the weather changed suddenly. There were fierce storms at sea, and a huge storm developed above the hills around the valley. The sky went as black as pitch and rain fell in an almost solid sheet. Within minutes the streams that enter the valley were swollen and before they knew what was happening, the people working above ground here at the mines were wading in six inches of water."

"This water had to go somewhere and it began to pour down the mine shafts, where around one hundred and fifty men and boys were working. The water pouring in forced air through the shafts and tunnels with such force it blew out all the lights. Because of course it were all candles then. The workers at the faces were in total darkness and water poured in on top of them or burst through loose rocks and boarding with terrific pressure. Those above ground did all they could, but the water was filling the mine too quickly."

"Eventually, some workers began to appear from below ground, covered in mud and gasping for air. There were heroes and tales of desperate attempts to save lives, but to the families there was a real fear that very few would come out alive. As the minutes turned to hours, miners were still making their way to the surface. The frightened and helpless people above ground kept vigil through the pouring rain, not knowing if they'd ever see their loved ones again. All through the night, men and boys somehow managed to climb out, through tunnels deep with water, up wooden ladders that were in the middle of waterfalls, from two hundred feet down and more. But the time between survivors appearing got longer and longer."

The Guide continued, relishing the chance to be as dramatic as possible. David was totally immersed in the tale.

"Towards the end of the next day, the rain started to ease and the flow of water into the shafts slowed enough to get more rescuers down. Soon they were bringing up bodies, two and three at a time. Drowned in mud most of them, others crushed under falling rocks and timber. Some survivors were retrieved too, little miracles! But soon, there was no thing more to be done. Out of the hundred and fifty men and boys down the pit at the time, just fifty-six came out alive. The rest were dead...some were never recovered..."

David knew. "A small boy aged 10 or 11!"

"That's right," the Guide said, a little puzzled, his Cornish face screwed up for a moment and David thought he saw a tear appear in the old man's eyes. "There was a boy called Jack Brandon working with three other men. Some survivors reported seeing them, struggling to keep their heads above the water. One of the three men, Peter Mellors, could be heard urging them, *'Stay above the seam',* but they were swept away by the force of the water as it burst through the shaft."

"Stay above the seam?" David was repeating words he'd heard before, almost, but now understood.

"Aye. The seam of silver on the face they were working. If they'd got above it, maybe they'd have made it."

"And they were never found?"

"That's right. Just them four. Swept away by the water, probably ended up well below ground; underground rivers could've picked 'em up..."

"And transported them closer to the coast?" David was thinking aloud.

"As likely a place as any. Rivers run to the sea." The Guide seemed to have enjoyed the chance to tell the full story. "There weren't a family in the village hadn't lost someone in the disaster. And the heart went out of the village and it died."

"Died?"

"A village isn't its buildings or its mines or factories. It's the folk as lives there. And these folk had their heart pulled out. This mine was one of many in the Trelloworron Valley. But the village that supplied much of its workforce had been decimated. Of course the mine itself also picked up some sort of stigma. No one would come to work here from outside. The village and the mine all but ran out of people. Many years later, the villagers that remained decided to change the village name to what it is today, and life did begin to come back to the place - even though the mine had closed anyway...but because of simple economics though, not anything else."

"So what's the village called now?"

"St. Eval!" The Guide replied chirpily, "and before, it was..."

"St. Evil!" The Guide nodded at David's astute guess. "But Saint Evil...?" David began to inquire.

"A corruption of an early Spanish name, from what I can gather, Saint Evilla. After the defeat of the Armada, many Spanish sailors were washed up in Cornwall and many settled here. Like most things at that time the words got confused..."

David thanked the old man and rose to his feet. Now it was all so clear. He left the guide and somehow stumbled his way around the grass to catch up with his parents.

"You look pale, David, are you all right?" His Mum was concerned.

David hardly heard her. He had solved the puzzle: "*Stay above the seam!*" That's what the voices had said; the ghost boy had been writing 'St. Evil' because he came from the mine at that village; the torrential rain had carried the bodies underground and trapped them - perhaps somewhere between the Prince Albert Hotel and The Dragon's Lair...*The Lair!* The huge cave, the place the underground river would have come to, had it not been turned into a huge crater by the same storm that swept the bodies from the mine deeper underground, never to reach open water.

He had done all this. Found it out. Alone. And Truddi hadn't been here to discover it with him. And she wasn't here to hear him unload the shattering revelations. She wasn't here!

~~~CHAPTER TWELVE~~~

Revelation

The serpent stood on the sandy shore of the sea.
Revelation; 12:18

The beach was full - it was going to be for the rest of the day. Truddi had checked in for the Surfing Contest and now sat with hoards of other wet-suited surfers, waxing their boards ready for the competition to start.

Truddi's parents found somewhere to sit, but Truddi disappeared in the mass of young people, assembling and shuffling around the beach like a gathering of seals. Weather conditions were perfect and she found herself with a group of Cornish teenagers, keen to help the 'Aussie Girl' with their knowledge of the local surf.

They laughed and joked for much of the morning as the competition progressed in other age groups, then they allowed themselves some practice time. The salt tasted good on her lips and she discovered just how much she'd missed surfing. David and the ghosts were at the back of her mind and the welcome attention of Stan and Paul encouraged her to relax. They practised for an hour or so, and then gave themselves a break as their heats approached.

She kept herself ready by slipping out and catching an occasional crest away from the judging area, mindful not to interfere with surfers on their scoring 'rides'. Truddi took the opportunity to practice the recent tips she'd been given. Then, contestants for the 'Girls 16 and under' section were called and she made her way to the section of the beach roped off for contestants.

The Head Judge gave the dozen or so girls the same talk he'd given to other groups already that day: "A surfer must execute the most radical controlled manoeuvres in the critical section of a wave with speed and power throughout. The surfer who executes such manoeuvres on the biggest and or best waves for the longest functional distance shall be deemed the winner."

Truddi knew this; she'd surfed in enough contests to know the score. She would have no problem with her stand-up surfing, and she inspected her fellow competitors to assess where the threats might come from. She also knew that the points in any competition are always won with 'airs' – using the wave to propel you and the board as high as possible to achieve and complete a recognised move.

She had a good range of air moves but so much depended on the waves. She lacked real knowledge of the waves she could expect at this beach. Her short practises already told her there were key differences here to the waves she had experienced in the tiny coves near The Prince Albert.

She knew surfing. She knew the critical section of the wave is the 'pocket', closest to the curl. The degree of commitment and risk involved in performing a manoeuvre close to the curl is the reason that it scores higher. Generally, the most critical section of a wave is the first section, known as 'out the back' or 'outside'.

But the only thing that was important right now was knowing she had to gain possession of the 'shoulders' of three good waves and surf in a good enough style to make it to the final. Her time in the water ended after she had picked three of the best rollers available and had good runs on all three. Her board skimmed along the waves and she was in perfect control each time.

Within moments of her stepping ashore after her third run, one of the organisers informed her of her progress to the final. She jumped for joy and felt Stan and Paul give her a quick hug of congratulations.

"That was crazy! That backside Ollie on your first run was sweet!" Stan was always over the top, but she knew his compliment was sincere.

"Thanks. But did you see those two Stale Fish on the last run? I thought the wave was never gonna end!" Truddi found herself hugging Paul, out of gratitude for the advice on wave selection.

She waved to her Mum and Dad who were standing in the distance, clapping. Just for a moment, she thought she saw David, but quickly realised that it couldn't have been him.

Now she had to wait most of the afternoon for the finals to start. After talking to her parents for a while, she returned to her new friends. She unzipped her wetsuit and pulled it down to her hips. She slapped some suntan oil where her bikini top didn't cover and lay on the sand to soak up some sun. Paul fancied himself as a bit of a clown and thought it funny to drop a bit of his ice-lolly onto her warm tummy.

"So Truddi…is there anyone back at home waiting for you?" Paul had so much confidence, Truddi felt caught up in all his plans. He had told her all he planned to do, travel, base-jumping, diving. Now he gave her a look that confirmed his intentions.

"I don't even know where home is, Paul. But no, there's no one…anywhere!"

They talked for most of the afternoon - but Truddi was constantly itching to get back into the sea. Under the pretence of practise, she made several trips into the waves and she almost missed the announcement of the start of the finals.

Her parents had found a new place to sit, closer to the action now that some space was appearing with the elimination of many of the contestants. They gave her a big 'thumbs up' as she made her way to the start. She smiled bigger than ever and waved confidently back. There were five other girls in her final, each with the task of finding enough wave time to get into the medals.

Truddi was relaxed and enjoying herself and her Australian experience gave her the edge over some of the contestants who were naïve. Truddi spotted waves early and got into good positions to gain possession of the waves, rising to her feet on the board just as her opponents made their move for the wave.

She was totally immersed in concentration as she paddled out on her board, waiting for one more wave, one more 'pocket' to send her on her way.

This one! She committed herself to the wave – the judges like to see that, and she threw in two quick chop-hops below the lip. *Get points on the cards quickly!*

She stood on her board and the wave carried her forward, gathering speed, staying ahead of the white water that pursued her. Her face tingled with salt and sand and her usually shiny hair was a mass of tangled, damp wool. But her brown eyes gleamed at the thrill of the chase. She could have surfed all night.

As the pocket gave her increased impetus she went for the big one. *Stale Fish!* The board left the water and she put her back hand down, cleanly grabbing the rail near her heel.

It was a perfect moment. As if time had stopped and held her there, her positioning was perfect, and from the judging box they must have seen pale blue sky between the water and her board. *Kill me now!* She thought. *I've done it all!*

Paul and Stan stood by her as she watched the judges under a sun canopy; they passed their findings on to the announcer.

Truddi was awarded third place, behind two local girls a little older than her. There was no shame in third and she accepted the prize as if it was an Olympic Gold Medal.

She could hear her parents' proud applause above all others and Stan gave her a peck on the cheek as an extra consolation. The kiss on her lips from Paul was more sensual and seemed to go on forever.

"You should have won!" He said, but Truddi knew he was only flattering her to improve his chances of getting serious with her.

"No," she said. "Did you see that girl who did the Inverted Air on the backside? She was good!"

She left her trophy with her parents and returned to some fun surfing. Stan and Paul had both made the finals of the 'Boys 14-16 category', but didn't get placed amid very good competition.

The three of them surfed for a few more hours while the remaining finals were played out. The beach began to empty as contestants and their families departed, some with prizes, some in tears.

She enjoyed the company of Stan and Paul. They never stopped smiling. The sea made her whole body feel alive. This was who she was, not some dowdy ghost-hunter. She felt like a young girl again. They splashed around in the sea and Paul used every opportunity to lift her up and throw her backwards into the sea. It was fun. A game! She wasn't stupid though and she'd noticed how he looked at her. It made her feel special.

Truddi's Dad called her from the top of the beach. They had a long drive back and wanted a meal before they left. Stan wished her well and Paul became quite slushy, wondering if they would ever meet again.

"Let's have your address, then. We can see what happens." Truddi suffered from the Australian trait of not beating about the bush. It took Paul a little by surprise but he eagerly agreed. He scribbled his details on a piece of paper when they got back to their bags on the beach. Then he took the bull by the horns.

"What about a kiss?"

Truddi nodded. Paul was definitely her type. They embraced and their salty lips met. His hands moved around her body and she sensed that Paul was getting a bit carried away. She removed herself from his clasp and said her goodbyes, both of them promising to keep in touch.

She held her Third Place Trophy all the way back to the hotel and fell asleep in the car thinking how proud David would be. Her dreams travelled as fast as their car, faces and memories illuminated by the headlights of her mind. Dreams of surfing turned to dreams of Paul. She felt herself wanting to dream of David, but something else invaded her dreams of Cornish summer...something darker.

There she was, sitting at her dressing table, writing with lipstick on the mirror. As she circled around herself in her dream, she saw that it wasn't words in red this time, written in lipstick on the mirror, but a coiling snake with red eyes, that wrapped itself around her own reflection. A deep voice resonated inside her and tried to eat at her insides.

"This is my home. I will destroy you if you return!"

As the words interrupted her breathing, almost jarring her from her sleep, she saw the face of the girl singer in the band, and the Lizard charm she had given her, which rose in the sky enveloped in golden light.

"Two doors...two doors..." *What did that mean?* Truddi woke confused. *I have a key. I have a key!* She took some comfort in the fact, but was uncertain still of what it all meant.

~~~CHAPTER THIRTEEN~~~

The Secret of the Ghoul

A monstrous serpent, Python, who was the son of Gaia (the goddess of the earth), haunted the caves of Parnassus until Apollo slew it with his first arrows. Apollo founded the Pythian Games to commemorate this victory and was afterwards named Apollo Physius. The monster's defeat was celebrated every nine years at the festival of Stepteria at Delphi and involved an enactment of the whole event.

"You went where?" David was annoyed.

"Newquay. To a surfing contest...I..."

"Surfing? So why couldn't you tell me?"

"You'd have made me choose between surfing and you! I needed to do this...I came..."

"So you'd sooner go to a beach than be with me? Why don't you go to a beach today? I'm sure you'll have a great time!"

"If I did go, you could come too."

"I don't think so...!"

"I didn't expect this reaction..." Truddi slapped her hand in frustration on the bed.

"I can't believe you put surfing before me."

Truddi had tried to placate him, but this was going nowhere. "No David...for my entire holiday, I've put you before my surfing!" She got up and made to go. "You're stubborn and selfish!"

Her words struck a chord with David. "I'm sorry," he said, before she could reach the door and leave.

She stopped and turned to face him slowly. "I came third...I won a prize..."

He smiled. "That's good. I'm proud of you. We've won something else too," he said. But he made a point of letting her tell him everything she'd done the day before.

She made the sea sound fun and exciting. Yet his stomach still knotted with each mention. He wasn't aware that she skirted around the subject of Paul and Stan. All the time he couldn't wait to tell her about the mine at St. Eval. Now they knew what they were dealing with...who they were dealing with.

"David, that's brilliant!" She lit up with a huge smile. He could tell he'd wiped all thoughts of sea and surfing from her mind. He had her back to himself again, devoted to solving his riddles.

For a moment, a fleeting second, something to do with the way she spoke about the ghosts, made him see her in a different light. Instead of vibrant and smiling, she became some doddery female detective from TV, shuffling around spooky houses and wearing tweed suits and glasses on the end of her nose. *That would be a tragedy!* He thought.

"Truddi?" He interrupted some intense argument Truddi was putting forward for the strange events they found themselves embroiled in. "If you ever want to go surfing again, you don't have to ask me or even consider me. You know? You do it if you want to."

She cocked her head to one side and regarded him for a moment. Then she smiled and lifted a hand and touched his cheek very gently. "You know, David. You are a *very* strange little boy!"

He smiled back at her.

"Where was I?" She retraced her thoughts. "Yes, as I was saying, before I was so politely interrupted, the decoy angle. The whatever-it-is-man with his coffin. I'm convinced we're being tricked. We can't find the boy, who we now know was lost in a flooded mine, because some 'force' doesn't want us to." *A very threatening and hateful force.* "We're being tricked and we need to turn our attention to you-know-who!"

The night was thick with excitement. They knew who had been calling them. They were sure they'd found the reason why the ghost of Jack Brandon and his fellow miners were lost, so far from their home village, yet they still didn't know how to find their lost bodies. David was on as big a roll with theories as Truddi had been on her surfboard.

"We have a boy whose body has never been buried, right?" He surmised. Truddi nodded. "And we have a weirdo who walks around at night pulling a coffin, right?" Truddi agreed and she turned the Lizard charm over in hand repeatedly, as if it offered her protection from demons she didn't want to think about. "So...I say, this monster has found the boy's body and kept it in the coffin!"

"Why?"

"Why? Because he's some sort of vampire...living off the dead..."

"I think that's ridiculous!" Truddi found it hard not to laugh too much and she could see that David was about to fall out with her about it.

"So you explain him!"

"I can't...but that doesn't make him a vampire!"

"One way to find out!"

~ ~ ~ ~

The lift shuddered gently as it came to a halt.

"Basement! Menswear, hardware, gifts and...er...shoes!" Truddi grinned again.

"How come you don't seem to know fear?" Little did David know the true answer to his question.

"How..? This plan of yours David, scares me to death. Can you come up with something better?"

He grinned, yet he felt a wave of bravado that he didn't want to stem. They left the lift and walked to the old wooden door that led to the tunnel.

"I'll wait here for him to come through. You stay up top," David instructed Truddi. "If I don't come back within an hour, get help."

"You're sure you're okay with this? Staying down here alone in the dark?" Truddi held the lift door open, offering him one last chance to change his mind. "Don't get me wrong, I like this part of the plan, you in the dark, damp, subterranean passage and me in the kitchen, but are you sure it's the only way?"

"We have to see what he's up to. We can't get in the lift with him. I'll be okay. Just because I'm afraid of the sea, doesn't mean I'm scared of everything else!"

She shrugged her shoulders and closed the lift door. There were clunks of machinery and whirring of gears and the lift ascended. David squinted to adjust his eyes to the dark and settled himself behind some old crates. He could smell the sea on them. That was worse than the dark.

David had been squatting behind them for about half an hour and was just beginning to get cramp when the lights in the passage came on with a loud clang of a circuit switch.

The passage was a store room and although lights had come on, they were too few to illuminate the whole room.

If he's a creature of the night, why does he need the lights on? David pondered for a moment then made sure he couldn't be seen in his hiding place.

He heard the scraping sound coming up the stone steps on the other side of the door that led to the tunnel. Eventually the huge wooden door opened and the tall, dark shape pulling the 'coffin' passed within feet of David's terrified face. The man left the 'coffin' in sniffing distance of David's face and went to call the lift.

When the lift doors opened, they threw light onto the man's swollen features - and also on David's hiding place. He ducked down, for fear that the light would pick him out. When he heard the lift doors shut and the lift move upwards, he peered out from his hiding place. The man was gone, probably to check out the hotel, but his 'coffin' was still here.

David had come prepared. With a wooden mallet and a pointed stake in his hands, he crept over to the box. He knelt beside it. Crazy as it was, he knew the boy's body was inside, denied a proper burial, held in limbo by this fiend. Maybe the brutal act of driving a stake through his heart would finally release him.

Close up, the box was less like a coffin than he'd first thought, but still he carefully prized the lid off and clutched his tools. The lid slid back and David raised the spike in his right hand, preparing to plunge it into the body in the casket. His mouth dropped open on seeing the contents and his eyes went white with realisation.

Behind him, the lift doors opened and the grotesque face of the huge man loomed over his shoulder.

"What do you want?" The man's voice out of the silence almost stopped David's racing heart.

"I'm sorry...I..." The man laid a hand on David's shoulder. "I thought you...I wanted to know what was in the box."

"Now you know!" The man said, a crooked smile spreading across his thick lips.

~~~~

Now he knew! Bottles of whisky, brandy, vodka, gin, boxes of cigarettes, chocolates, cheese.

"I'm a smuggler...is all." David noticed how the man had a pleasant manner, despite his deformity, which had indeed been made to appear worse by the angles of the lights and the severe shadows they cast. Close up, David began to find him quite jolly. "It still goes on you know. Things are cheaper elsewhere - I bring stuff in...The hotel can always use some spirits."

Spirits? David felt the need to tell all. The man, who gave David his name as Mr Lacey, sat on his box of contraband and listened to David's talk of storms and mining disasters. He chuckled once or twice, but never once did he doubt what David was telling him was the truth.

When Truddi saw them both come out of the lift together she gasped. David was quick to put her at ease and although she found it hard to look at Mr Lacey for a time, her fears were soon dispelled.

"He has acromegaly, Truddi."

"Acro..?" Truddi spluttered.

"...Megaly." David smiled at Mr Lacey who laid a huge hand on top of David's head and gently tousled his hair.

"I can seem scary, I know. But most people around here knew me before the disease kicked in." Mr Lacey explained about the disorder, which most commonly affects middle-aged adults. How it is hard to diagnose and frequently missed. How he had planned a career in software development and how he had to give it up.

"He's a smuggler!" Enthused David.

"One who's going to get caught if I don't move the merchandise soon." Mr Lacey grinned and Truddi's body finally relaxed, the last of her fears visibly lifting from her.

The door opened suddenly behind her and there stood the Hotel owner, Mr Kirkman. He was tightening the belt on his dressing gown and on seeing Truddi and David he looked like a frightened rabbit caught in the headlights of a speeding car. Mr Lacey waved a hand in his direction, telling him not to worry and Mr Kirkman relaxed, happy that he would have no explaining to do.

The four of them moved the contraband and re-stocked the hotel's spirit store. The illegality of it all didn't concern Truddi or David. They were happy that this was as sinister as the episode had been.

"So...what was the tunnel for?" David asked Mr Lacey.

"Back in the days when only rich people 'ad 'olidays, it was built as a short-cut to the beach from the hotel. Rich folk have legs and never use them...you notice that?" Mr Lacey was as kind and good-natured as his face was distorted, and both Truddi and David had quickly warmed to him.

With four of them working hard the smuggled goods were soon stored and it was time to go.

"Now remember...you've not seen me...I don't exist...you know?" said Mr Lacey, after they'd put everything back in its place. Mr Kirkman gave them both a look of gratitude and then led Mr Lacey away for his payment. And when they'd gone, Truddi and David reflected on the chatter and the local tales that Mr Lacey had told them, and they now knew all about an annexe to the tunnel that led in the direction of 'The Dragon's Lair', which had been closed ever since a rock fall in September 1847. The time of the great storm!

It was too dangerous to even think about going through the annexe. Never go down there! Mr Lacey's warnings were precise.

David and Truddi agreed they'd go down there tomorrow!

~~~CHAPTER FOURTEEN~~~

Brothers

Thy shape,
Like his, and colour Serpentine, may show
Thy inward fraud;

Paradise Lost, Book X, Milton

As they walked along the tunnel the next day, they were relaxed and eager. In truth they were casual, as if they were strolling around the pretty streets of Morullion. They came across a slight curve in the direction of the otherwise straight tunnel and at the limits of the torch beam, noticed the pattern of tiles change, high in the wall. It could mean only one thing - the original location of the second tunnel, the annexe that led to 'The Dragon's Lair'.

Tucked into the bend and constantly in darkness, it was easy to see how it could go unnoticed all these years. Truddi turned on her torch. A brick wall had been built to shield the tunnel entrance. Before they felt the first pangs of disappointment, David had already noticed the dampness of the floor where they stood. He pulled at one of the bricks on the leading edge and it moved away with ease. The mortar was too soft to hold them.

The wall came down in only minutes, whole sections giving way at once. Now they were confronted by a solid looking door - like the one at the very head of the tunnel entrance and they knew only too well how stout that one was. But David again seemed to sense its fallibility. At least to half way up, the door was rotten and it gave way without protest. Only then to reveal an iron bar gate.

"They don't mean anyone going down here, do they!" said David.

Truddi was already at work, using a brick and some of the stronger wood to lever the lower bars on the gate. The stonework that held the bars began to crumble and between them they managed to force an opening at ground level, wide enough to crawl through.

"I knew I'd had too much clotted cream!" David gasped as he found himself wedged. Truddi grinned and pulled him through, ignoring his yelping as bits of him dragged and snagged on rocks and iron bars. There were no lights in this bit of tunnel and the blackness was at first overwhelming. Truddi pointed her torch ahead and then screamed in horror.

The light had shone on the face of the boy, now known by them both to be Jack Brandon. He was faded around the edges, barely visible in some places and appeared totally dejected.

"Jack? You're Jack aren't you?" David spoke first. He didn't know if ghosts could hear. But Jack spoke in return.

"I'm dead...aren't I."

Truddi and David had never considered that a ghost wouldn't realise that its natural life had ended.

"For one hundred and sixty years!" David didn't mean to be blunt. Jack looked down and sobbed.

"Feels like we just got trapped down 'ere - only a couple o' days ago." He couldn't speak any more. David and Truddi walked past him and came across a pile of rocks that blocked the tunnel. Jack passed through their bodies, leaving an icy chill that brought back a twinge of remembered apprehension for Truddi. Jack's ghost dissolved through the side of the tunnel. They moved to the spot he'd passed through and David began to pull loose rocks away.

"Keep the torch on here, I can't see what I'm doing," moaned David.

"Sorry," the light fell onto the area he was working on, then moved again, "I just can't believe this place. It's huge! I can't see all of it."

David gave up expecting to have light and worked in the darkness, desperate to follow the route Jack Brandon had just taken.

Their torchlight lit only small parts of their environment; fleeting glimpses of black rock, shimmering with water that seeped from above. Their other senses filled in the darkness, imagining boulders and rock-fall debris, hearing whispered warnings and deathly cries, smelling sea-salt and decay.

David finally pushed against a large rock which moved and caused a small rock-fall behind it, creating a gap he could squeeze through. He wasted no time. Truddi followed.

Now it was David's turn to freeze. He was perched on a narrow stack of boulders, but only feet below him he could hear, feel, taste, smell...the sea. Until Truddi arrived alongside with the torch, the cave was totally black. Even with the torch on the entire cavern wasn't visible all at once. The sea was bursting in through cracks and fissures very close by, although they couldn't see it and the cavern echoed like a cathedral with the rumblings of waves breaking into cliffs a long way off.

In the narrow beam of Truddi's torch, Jack's body glided over the subterranean sea, his silver aura like shattered moonlight on the waves. He landed opposite them, across perhaps fifty metres of gurgling sea. Jack sat next to a small pile of bones on a ledge of rocks just above the churning black water. He looked at David and Truddi and then at the skeleton. It had to be his. He sobbed a while, and then pleaded.

"Take me home...to St. Evil, please..."

As he faded, a sudden breeze seemed to rock the bones. Truddi scanned the ledge and they both squinted to make out three other sets of bones. Water and wind seemed to squeal from every direction. They could see a small waterfall depositing water from an underground stream high on the wall opposite. Shadows of white water blew out from gaps in the rocks in every direction. Winds blew through pipe holes as water pushed the air in front of it. The howling became like church organ music and David was noticeably apprehensive.

"I'm sure the water's rising!" He'd been brave to be this close to the sea. But the truth was he had frozen. He clung to the rocks, unable to move.

"You'll be all right, David. Try to laugh it off!"

Instead, David suddenly screamed in panic. He clawed at the rock wall behind him. "You don't know...you don't know. My brother's dead...what did I do?"

Truddi felt water lap at her ankles as the water level in the cavern started to rise. They were going to have to be quick. She could see that David though was on the verge of facing up to something he'd hidden away inside for so long. She placed a hand on his arm.

"It's all right," she said softly, "tell me what happened."

David struggled to speak, to give voice to the images that haunted him every day. Images he tried to hide from, to keep out of his mind.

Now, once again, he would have to live through that fateful day. Here, back in Cornwall. Here, so close to where it all happened. Here, with the same sea gathering around him to make sure he told the truth this time; told it as it really happened.

The sun was shining and the sound of happy laughter echoed somewhere behind them in the cove. And there was his brother, playing in the summer sea. David looked back through time and saw his own image emerging from the waves and laughing with delight. He saw his brother, concerned at first for David, then...words began to come.

"When you surf, do you know what bit of water to look for?"

"The pocket, just before the curl. The water is moving fastest there."

"Does it hurt you if it hits you?"

"Sometimes, if it comes off the shoulder and you're not expecting it, but on the board it normally pushes you. It's worse if you're static. Like just standing there."

David painted a picture of that summer day. Stevie standing in the sea up to his chest; the tug of the water as the sea left the shore and the water pulling him down, fixing him to the spot. He turned around only to see the swell towering over him.

Stevie was aware of the iron fist of the sea hovering behind him, preparing to strike like a cobra or serpent. In the same moment that his eyes found his brother David, safe near the beach, he knew instinctively that an immense force of nature had been turned on him. It was this awesome power that slapped into the back of Stevie's head.

He didn't really feel it. He lost consciousness, though only for a moment, the same water reviving him that gushed down his throat. He tried to put his feet down, to find something solid to support him whilst he gathered himself. Instead he felt his feet push through the waves above him. He tried in vain to correct his attitude and his lungs cried out for air to replace the sea water that filled them. The sea wanted nothing less than an emphatic victory; the total humiliation of its erstwhile tormentors. Stevie was flotsam in a turbulent current. The sea then pressed Stevie into a rock and then span and twisted him like washing in a machine.

"You can't know this!" Truddi held his hand, her eyes glancing down at the water lapping at her feet.

"I know it, Truddi. I've seen it every time I closed my eyes. I have been Stevie in those moments. I know what drowning feels like. I know what the sea wants to do to people."

He continued, his voice projecting the imagery around them both.

David had laughed at first. How many times had Stevie disappeared under crashing foam? The echoes of David's initial reaction had haunted his whole life ever since. He re-lived in his dreams the ghostly image of Stevie, all the life squeezed out of him, and the sound of the sea replaced by his own manic laughter.

"My brother was dying...I was laughing. Don't you see? I laughed when Stevie died. My own brother..." David couldn't control his tears. The floodgates were open. "What does that make me? How can I ever laugh again?"

"It wasn't your fault...you were a child. You have to stop blaming yourself. You have to remember the times you and Stevie laughed together." Truddi shifted her weight from foot to foot, anxiously testing the water depth. "David, the water level is rising and we have a task to do." She kissed

David on his tear-soaked cheek. "I'll swim across, you can hold the torch."

Truddi had already gone, into the water like an otter. David shone the torch for her as she swam to the other side, a good fifty metres. She swam well, then hauled herself out of the water and climbed out onto the other side, where she sat herself between the bones.

She pulled out large plastic bags from a smaller bag strapped to her waist. The first bin liner was for Jack. Without ceremony, she dumped his remains into the bag, pausing only for a moment to look at the skull. David heard her whisper a prayer to Jack and told his empty eye sockets that he'd soon be home.

~~~~

It was harder than she expected to swim back. And David couldn't move to help her lift the bag out of the tumultuous sea. She bobbed in the water, kicking her legs and doing her best to stop the sea from crashing her into the rock face. She raised the bag as high as she could but she needed help to lift it out completely. Strong as she was, her energy was being sapped.

"David..." she spluttered, "come on...take it...it's Jack's body...he came to you for help..."

David moved, carefully. Truddi was treading water, spitting mouthfuls out at a time. He leaned over as much as he dare and took the bag from her. She smiled at him, trying to instil him with some self-belief, and then swam back to the other side to fetch another set of bones.

David noticed the water level creeping higher and the crashing and exploding of water on rock echoed like thunder inside the cavern. He clung tighter to the narrow ledge he was on and squeezed the bag of bones through the hole they'd come through without taking his back from the wall.

Truddi couldn't find many bones of the three remaining miners and managed to fit them into a single bag. She swam towards the shaky torchlight but the weight of the bag in the rough water began to tire her. It felt as if the sea was fighting her. She had won a trophy for beating the waves, but now it wanted to fight, to make her struggle. The harder she swam, the further away David and his light seemed to be.

Her face went under for a second or two, and she spat water as she emerged. For a moment she was confused. David's light seemed a long way off now, and it appeared to dance and flicker.

Then she knew it wasn't David's torch. Around the cavern, several weak lanterns flickered for a moment, as if the other miners were watching the recovery of their lost bodies. She made out their faces and tried to tell them in her mind that she was helping them. The miners dissolved, leaving her searching for David's light once more.

Suddenly, her body became intensely cold. She had a sensation that something evil was in the cavern with them. She took a deep breath and swam hard for David's torch.

David appeared more confident now. His tears had stopped and the mere fact that he'd spoken about the nature of his horror and guilt over Stevie's death had seemed to lift his soul a little. He was able to stand on the rocks, his ankles under the lapping water. From there, he lifted the second bag out of the water and then helped Truddi back onto the ledge.

They stood, looking at each other and she began to smile. Her clothes were wet and heavy around her and she felt inwardly cold.

A shriek of wind seemed to howl up from the hollows in the dark cavern. The rising sound was of a rush of air or water and even the sea seemed to still itself to hear better.

Something silver caught Truddi's eye and she turned to see the spectre of one of the miners, Peter Mellors, his body twisted as if straining to hold on to something. His face grimaced with pain, fear and sadness. He skimmed at great speed across the black water right towards them.

"Stay above the seam!" The voice echoed around the cavern and repeated several times. Then, as he halted, right alongside Truddi, he turned his face, seemingly at her, but looking beyond her, through her. His voice changed. Deeper. Commanding. Warning.

"Stay above the seam!"

The miner's appearance changed. His eyes glowed red and huge; the face became that of an animal perhaps, or a demon and then became featureless. A black mass, not of substance but of emptiness itself.

"I am the serpent and I will devour you, girl!"

Truddi felt the words again, resonating inside her chilled soul. Oblivious to anything other than her own fear, she groaned as the serpent dissolved around her. Within seconds, the whole cavern shook with the thunderous impact of a large wave and water spouted from even the tiniest of vents. Behind them, some of the rocks they'd moved to open up the chamber, slipped and the exit was blocked, and Truddi, in shock at the sudden appearance of the beast, lost her footing on the quaking rocks and fell backwards into the water, taking the torch with her.

"No!" David threw out a hand but it was too late. He saw her drop like a stone into the violent water. The torch fell slowly alongside her, illuminating her through the turbulent sea like a flickering old home movie. His face contorted with horror as her right arm and leg became entangled in some sort of old cable, possibly lighting cable from the old tunnel annexe. Truddi struggled in the water beneath him for a moment, fixing her eyes on him, kicking upwards but to no avail. She was trapped!

The torch continued to fall past her, and soon she was nothing more than the silhouette of an underwater marionette.

The Serpent's coils entwined her, pulling tighter around her arm and leg, tugging her towards the bottom of the cavern. Who knew how deep it was? Its depths had already swallowed the last of the light. Her eyes battled the murky water to find a way of releasing herself. Her left hand tried to free the right from the slithering coils. As the Serpent dragged her downwards it shared with her some of itself. Ageless. Peerless. A worm of the inner depths of the world. A manifestation of base emotions, hungry for 'food'.

As she drifted downwards, she saw in the strata of rock that formed the cavern those rocks that were once far below the sea bed, and had been long since thrust upwards to form the Lizard Peninsula. There contained in the geology was the pre-history of the world in the blink of a red eye.

"You will play no part."

Truddi felt her lungs cry out. She couldn't hold her breath much longer. She wondered at her destiny that the Serpent sought to deny. It was no accident she had travelled half way around the world on the way to somewhere else and met David. It was no accident she had become involved in the search for those who couldn't rest. And if such things had meant to be then she knew there must be an alternative to spending an eternity in the presence of something so foul her soul railed against it. She kicked hard once more and felt the Serpent wince in pain.

The Serpent's head appeared close to hers. Several tongues flicked at her face and she felt them lash at her cold skin, burning and poisonous. He sneered at her and she saw in the plumbless depths of his eternal eyes the misery and venom of the world, brewing in vast cauldrons in the pit of the earth, ready to serve the world in return for the Serpent's entertainment and nourishment.

She succumbed.

Only to be alerted by four faint lights that seemed to dance around her. Four flickering candles on the headbands of long dead Cornish miners.

She saw them, Jack Brandon, Peter Mellors, Daniel Kennaughton and Michael Pawley. She knew them in an instant. She saw their drama unfold, their fear as the water rose around them; Mellors urging his friends up the slippery wall, trying to hold them above the seam. She saw the heroism of the men as they sacrificed themselves to keep the young Jack Brandon's head above the water at the expense of their own.

She saw the seam of silver sparkle with the hatred and malice of the Serpent.

You can't have them! She thought. *They will go home!*

"And I will have you!"

Jack Brandon offered a hand to Truddi. So too did Peter Mellors and she found herself in their drama as it played out. They struggled to keep her alive. They would not see her drown. They struggled with their dying strength to raise her above the seam as the water poured over them and rose over their desperate faces.

She felt the Serpent weaken. And then she saw Stevie. She knew him from his photograph. He swam between the Serpent's head and hers, a smile on his face the radiance of which illuminated the murky water and stunned the Serpent. Then Stevie and the others were gone. She felt the coils slither from her limbs and loosen. Yet she had no strength left to finally pull free. She drifted motionless, ever deeper.

In her mind the Serpent sneered.

"I still have *him*!"

~ ~ ~ ~

David struggled to stand up. His shouts were mocking echoes that replayed his despair in a resounding din. The darkness suffocated him; he almost collapsed under the weight of the desperation he felt. He looked around for someone else, so that they might save her. He knew there could be no one. As his eyes focused back on Truddi in the last of the torchlight he felt a presence behind him. He steadied his breathing; tried to gather himself. Daring to move, to turn slowly, he began to speak.

"Stevie?" David wanted it so much to be his brother. Yet he found himself looking into the eyes of Jack Brandon. Sad eyes. Eyes that had been closed too soon. However, David felt with more certainty than ever before that his brother was there too. That he had latched on to Jack Brandon, another young boy whose life had been cut short. David looked beyond Jack Brandon's face, through him, until he could see Stevie's faint image glowing faintly in the dark of the cavern. He was there. He had been there all along. Forced to play a part for the Serpent to snare David and Truddi.

All the love and hugs he'd ever shared with Stevie, seemed to swim into his body. His brother loved him for all time. He knew that. There was no blame. No need for guilt. David's eyes filled with water of their own. Yet in that same moment, David felt that he'd changed; that the time had come to move on, and to let go.

Turning quickly, he dropped off the ledge and slipped feet first into the water. He took a deep breath and plunged into the water. Stevie would have to guide him. He could see nothing at all. He began to panic, to realise the enormity of what he was doing; to doubt he had the ability. Still, down he went.

His body told him how cold the water was. His senses told him of a malice, a threat that had a taste for the essence of human life. He knew in his bones it had all been a plan. Stevie, Truddi and he were all to die in this water. He choked again and fought the desire to turn back. Then his heart told him to go on and he felt Stevie's hand lead him down until his fingers touched Truddi's soft arm.

He worked quickly to prise the cable away from Truddi's entangled limbs and they both pushed up for the surface. He kicked hard and through the cloudy green of the dark sea, he could see her face, her eyes bulging and her mouth opening slowly, desperate for air. He knew the feeling. He had lived it for nine years. Her instincts to breathe would kick in and she would be unable to prevent herself from opening her lungs for another breath.

Then she would drown.

He put his hand under her chin forcing her mouth shut and her eyes pleaded with him to hurry for the surface. He used all his strength to push her for the surface and her head broke water in the same instant her mouth opened and drew in a lungful of air.

They spluttered together onto the rocks and struggled to bring other senses to bear. Truddi's choking and huge gasps for air created a cacophony in the chamber.

"You were caught in a cable."

She spluttered and vomited. Glancing back into the water she seemed to be looking for something that her eyes didn't want to see. David hauled himself onto the narrow pile of rocks they had been standing on. He trembled at what he had done and then took her arms and pulled her up.

"Thanks..." Truddi said, once she'd regained her breathing.

"Only temporary." David gestured at the closed up escape route. Even in their relief they knew they were still trapped by the rock fall, and were now in total darkness.

"You did well." Truddi breathed hard in the darkness, but he could tell her composure was returning.

David wanted to tell her about Stevie, that it was all over. The nightmare, the guilt, the sorrow. He would be able to move on and that just as Jack Brandon's ghost would find peace soon, the same would happen for Stevie one day.

But that would depend on them getting out of here themselves.

Truddi's breathing returned to normal. David listened, tried to make out the features on her face but it was too dark. He could do with seeing her smile right now.

"What are you thinking?" He asked. He'd settle for hearing her voice.

"I'm so confused. I was certain Mr Lacey was the threat. When he turned out to be a nice guy, I forgot all about it. We may have solved the part of the puzzle with Jack and the miners, but..."

"But what?"

"Nothing makes sense. There's something else going on, I'm certain. But what it is I have no idea. Just Jessica's warnings of decoys and, well..." There was a long silence and then she whispered, "The Serpent!"

"What? I didn't catch that..." But he didn't have time to get an answer.

They were both startled by a loud crashing that echoed around the cavern. They felt the water lapping at their ankles as it rose onto the ledge where they crouched. *I'm not ready to die!* Thought David as the darkness pressed down on him.

They braced themselves at the sound of more rocks falling. A shaft of light came through the rocks above them. The smiling and bulbous face of Mr Lacey peered into the cavern.

"Kids? You safe?"

They squealed in the affirmative. Mr Lacey inched his way inside and set his oil lamp down next to him.

"You two...not listening to me...they'll probably close my tunnel up for good now. How will that affect my business?" He smiled at them. David didn't for one minute believe he was prepared to put profit ahead of the potential safety of others. It was a certainty though; the authorities would find out and the tunnel would be sealed up for good because of this.

"You okay to get out?" Mr Lacey guided them to their feet and held them upright away from the clawing water.

"Sure," Truddi replied, "but we've got some friends with us!" She grabbed the two bags of bones and winked at David.

~~~CHAPTER FIFTEEN~~~

The Cemetery and the Seed

This ponder, that all nations of the earth
Shall in his seed be blessed: by that seed
Is meant thy great Deliverer, who shall bruise
The serpent's head; whereof to thee anon
Plainlier shall be reveal'd.

Paradise Lost, Book XII, Milton

The burial of Jack Brandon and the remains of the three other miners at the Parish Church of St. Eval was quite a media event. David and Truddi were heroes. Of course they failed to mention the trail of clues and supernatural happenings that led them to the bodies. Instead the 'official' story was of a chance discovery near The Dragon's Lair. They both failed to mention the tunnel from the Prince Albert Hotel and David and Truddi even helped Mr Lacey build a more secure wall to prevent anyone else from 'straying' into the annexe.

As the snapping of photographers began to die down, Truddi saw a familiar face in the crowd. She eased her way through the press and local dignitaries and approached the woman.

"You are quite a celebrity!" It was the lead singer from the band. She was dressed for an office job and wore narrow glasses. But the warmth she emanated was still there and she hugged Truddi like an old friend. "I couldn't believe it when I heard about you. I've been trying to be famous for years, you beat me to it!"

They both laughed, but Truddi had so many questions. They walked slowly into the graveyard away from everyone else.

"I can't go on calling you 'Band Girl'" said Truddi.

"Oh I don't know..." she giggled. "From now on, call me Sally."

"Do you know what I'm...involved with?" Truddi had to know. They stopped and Sally turned to face her.

"It's written in your eyes." Sally looked as grave as their surroundings. "I wish I could help you more. I wish I could carry the burden for you..."

Burden? This demonic serpent she had seen, the creature that spoke to her, warning her, had some real purpose. *A purpose known to others, is that it?* Somewhere in its threats it had seemed to believe that she had a purpose too. This adventure wasn't over for her.

So what was it that she had to do? The demon snake or whatever it was had returned to the depths of the world, but it scared her more than anything else. She had stumbled on a force of terror; one that knew her and didn't want her around. Finding Jack Brandon was a sub-plot, nothing more. This wasn't the end!

"The Serpent? Is it real?" Truddi struggled to make sense of it all. If it was real, why could no one help her?

"It's real. I came up against him in 1989. I was too young, really. My brothers took the brunt of his wrath." Sally's face filled with a long memory of pain. "We did no more than prick his pride. My brothers died within a year."

Truddi gulped back her horror.

"I kind of know when he's about," continued Sally, her face turned toward Truddi and trying to fill her with strength and courage. "And I see those who take the fight to him. It won't be you alone, Truddi."

"I don't think I can do this."

"It won't be your decision."

"I leave England soon. I'll be out of the whole thing!"

Sally looked at her for a moment. "I don't think so. I gave you an amulet because I can see you will be in the thick of the battle when it comes."

"I won't!" Truddi tried to sound emphatic, tears welling in her eyes. "I'm not going into...battle! It's not about me. I don't know how to use this charm you gave me. What is it for? What did you mean about 'two doors'?"

"I don't know, Truddi. That amulet, that message, those instructions are for you. When the time comes, you will know." With that, she turned and vanished among the headstones and the grey morning.

Truddi gathered herself, wiped her eyes and tried to find some resolve inside, a place where she could gather strength from. She looked back towards the church door and the thinning crowd. She saw David and noticed how straight he stood now. The smile was broad, the former melancholy now just a few subtle brush strokes on his face. She made her way back towards him. His eyes searched for her and the smile became a grin when their eyes met and he waved to her.

He had his victory. He had overcome so much. *It should be his fight, not mine!*

She thrust her hand into her pocket and her fingers stroked the familiar shape of the Lizard key charm. The ghost adventure was over, that was certain, but there was unfinished business for her. The Serpent was still around, and he was far from being Truddi's biggest fan. The death threats were bad enough. There was hate beyond her imaginings in them.

And yet she felt that she had allies...somewhere.

~~~~

For David, the nightmares had gone. He was relishing the chance to be a young boy once more.

The part that Truddi had played in resurrecting their son was not lost on Mr and Mrs Givens. Nor was it lost on David. But Canada is a long way away. For now though, as they emptied the car of the things they needed with them on the beach, all David could think of was walking along the shore with Truddi. Flasks and packed lunches were of little concern.

"Well," said Truddi, "if I tell girls in Canada how you English guys can thrill us, they'll be over here in a hurry...for sure!" She sat back on the rocks that made an ideal seat on the top of the cliffs. Her hair shone in the late afternoon sun and she leaned back to allow it to blow in the gentle breeze.

"You can't complain about England being dull, that's a fact!" David spoke, but his eyes were watching the horizon.

"I know what they'll ask me in Canada...and I'll do my best to tell them... but...I've not really had enough experience to know for sure..."

"Mmm?" David was barely listening.

"How good are English boys at kissing?" She smiled at him and made a gesture with her hands that seemed to urge him to get onto her wavelength.

"I don't know..."

"No...That's what the girls will ask me!"

"Right."

"I need to find out." This time her voice left him in no doubt.

"Right!" David smiled at her. They kissed as if they were born to it. If ever two people were matched, these two were. David loved everything about her, everything except where she was going to live. They looked deep into each other's faces and she smiled and gave him a final peck on the cheek. As she turned and moved a few steps away, she casually tossed a piece of paper from her pocket and Paul's address blew over the cliff unnoticed.

"I've got all the info I need. Now I can tell Canadian girls all about it." Truddi was all smiles. Her smile faded as she saw David's expression.

"You'll live in Canada, Truddi." As if that was a terrible illness or somewhere far away such as the moon. Truddi walked back to him, her eyes full of the strength and confidence that she was so full of, and that he loved her for.

"And what's that between us...it's only sea." She emphasised the point with a piercing stare of playful victory and once David had submitted, she span around and walked back towards the beach. "Coming?" She called over her shoulder.

"Yes...in a while." David watched her go then turned his attention back to the sea. Now he knew how it all worked, he hoped it wouldn't be long before some other boy or girl were given the task of finding Stevie's lost body and letting him rest.

He also knew that he carried Stevie with him and that he'd be there, at his side when he most needed him. And he was certain that Stevie could see him and he was proud of his little brother. *If tears fall from now on, they'll be tears of reassurance.* The first ones slipped from his eyes at that moment. "God bless, Stevie."

The world seemed all right, yet there was still this dull ache in the back of his head that had come on after his dream the other night. Sometimes it was truly painful and left him feeling swallowed by a heavy darkness, as if he was being pulled toward the centre of the earth. He winced as it gave him a sharp reminder but he made up his mind he wasn't going to be a wimp anymore. No need to worry his mother about it.

Pulling his shoulders back, David turned and set off after Truddi along the serpentine rocks to the beach, already planning a holiday in Canada.

The end.

ABOUT THE AUTHOR

Stuart Cresswell was born in Leicestershire, England and lived and worked there for most of his life until moving to Nova Scotia in 2006. He works as a film and TV Producer and Director but is continually striving to spend all day writing! The Lizard Tales is his first series of books, but he's written a number of stage plays and films and he is also the creator and writer of the "Cyborg Warriors" sci-fi comics.

In the next of

THE
LIZARD
TALES

A holiday on Cornwall's Lizard Peninsula with her 'geeky' cousin is a long way from the type of holiday Alona wanted. When she falls under the spell of a long-dead wrecker, lured by the promise of gold and power, Alona falls prey to an ever bigger evil.

Her cousin Jayne, and three unlikely heroes are all that stand between her and an eternity of servitude to the malignant Serpent of The Lizard.

Coming Soon!

THE GOLD OF
'BLACK' TREVALLIAN
Book Two of

THE
LIZARD
TALES

by

Stuart Cresswell

Read the opening of the new adventure now…

~~~CHAPTER ONE~~~

The returning

Her head pulsed with rage and burned with the imagined gazes of countless people as she slammed the door behind her and left the caravan. Alona paused for a moment, fought back tears of frustration, determined that no one should believe her defeated. She straightened her shoulders and deliberately set one foot in front of the other. Conscious that she didn't want to run lest she appeared afraid, she raised her head high in defiance and pride. Yet inside she knew the door could open behind her and she'd be drawn back into a confrontation she had no stomach for.

Her heel caught on the edge of the gravel track that swept down the hillside of the caravan park. In an instant she was flat on her face on the soft earth. The laughter of children playing nearby became the laughter of the whole world; laughing at her, Alona Marrye, the girl without a friend in the world.

In seconds she was on her feet. Her summer dress had largely escaped grass and mud stains, but her bare knees and shins had landed in a particularly soft patch of grass, and the soil beneath was moist and loose from recent rain. Worse still, her chin had hit the ground hard and she could already feel the throbbing expansion of a thick lip. Her cheeks were smeared with mud, which the tears of humiliation couldn't wash.

She ran as fast as her wobbly heel would allow up the slope towards the exit of the park. Past families, making their way to the beach or the pool, her drunken gait and flailing arms attracting more attention than she could bear. Yet she held on to the outburst of tears and sobbing that welled up inside. Held on as she hurried down the narrow lane from the caravan park to the nearby cove. Held tighter on to the boiling rage that accompanied the desperate feelings of humiliation, frustration…loneliness.

She'd never run so far in her life. Even when the track turned to sand she didn't stop. She let herself run from the track along a narrow path, overgrown and coarse with hardy bushes and shrubs. This she knew led to the cliff top. Away from people. Away from prying eyes. There, finally, she could cry.

She flung herself to the ground concealed by serpentine rocks and thorny bushes. Hidden there she began to wail and rant, throw her fists to the sky, sobbing until she could feel her temples pounding.

Now her eyes were sore. She was filthy. The babbling sound of a stream demanded her attention. She was hot. She'd run through the hottest part of the hottest day of the week so far. Her dress stuck to her and annoyed her. She needed to cool down. Glancing around her to confirm there was no one about, she slipped the dress from her shoulders and knelt at the side of the stream. Here it became wider and deeper, almost desperate to hang on to the cliff before disappearing through thorns and grassy rocks over the cliff edge and down to the sea.

The water was cool. It restored her inner strength. She scrubbed her face, using the stream's reflection as a mirror. She allowed her grip on her dress to loosen and she patted the cooling water onto her chest, mindless of the damage to her new bra.

Then, she felt a strange sensation as though unseen eyes were watching her. She looked around but saw no one. Nervously she pulled her dress up to her chest and her nostrils widened, sniffing the air for danger.

She was sure she heard something, a bird perhaps, deep in the thorn bushes. Or a snake! She slid backwards on her bottom, her eyes fixed on the bush. She pressed her back into a thick thorn bush and waited for her doom.

"Who's there? I can see you?" Imaginings of the worst kind ran through her head. Girls of her age were prey for certain men. Now she was really afraid. No reply came, but the bush behind her rustled. She was sure she felt breathing. She turned her head slowly. Among the leaves and thorns she could make out eyes. But the face seemed incomplete as if it was made from leaves itself.

She screamed and darted away, her legs carried her quickly now that her shoes were off. Then her foot touched nothing. In an instant she knew she'd gone too far. She hadn't been looking, hadn't realised how close to the edge of the cliff she was. She choked on a scream and knew that there was no way she could prevent herself from running over the edge. Then something caught her arm.

Her wrists were thin but the grip that held her seemed just as thin. It couldn't possibly prevent her from plummeting to her death on the rocks below. As if to answer her fear, a second grip attached itself around her waist. This was a rope and the tug on her midriff pulled the air from her chest. But she felt herself swinging back towards the safety of the cliff top. She landed with a clatter on top of a young boy in camouflage combats and his face beamed back at her from under green and black striped camo-paint.

Overcome with emotion at being saved she felt the need to kiss him. When she saw from his grinning face that the boy looked like he might enjoy it, she stopped herself and rolled off him. His long, thin fingers still held her wrist. The rope dropped from her waist as she unclasped his hand from her arm and rose to her feet. Another boy, identically dressed coiled the rope back neatly and placed it inside a utility belt.

A third boy emerged from the bush where she'd seen the eyes. He was stouter than the other two and wore a camouflage baseball cap over a mop of bright ginger hair. His camouflage face paint was unable to hide all of his freckles.

"You freak!" Yelled Alona, but her ire was met without a response. "Why were you spying on me?" Her tone had changed to a plea, only now did they look ready to speak.

"We weren't. We were on manoeuvres. We always come up here." The ginger one spoke with a husky voice that enabled to her to guess at his age. *Fourteen*, she thought. And the one on the floor, despite his face paint and military clothing was no more than thirteen. She had swallowed her fear now, regained her composure, her air of superiority. These people weren't worth her time.

The full story coming soon!